# GOING DOWN HARD

*NEW YORK TIMES BESTSELLING AUTHOR*

# CARLY PHILLIPS

Copyright © Karen Drogin 2017
Print Edition
CP Publishing 2017
Cover Photo and Design: Sara Eirew

**Billionaire Bad Boys: Rich, Powerful and sexy as hell.**

Derek West rose from poverty to take the tech world by storm. He's sexy, confident and has no problem making a play for the opposite sex. He never anticipates that the one woman who has him going down hard, is going to make this bad boy work for what he wants … and needs.

**"Carly Phillips is synonymous with red-hot romance and passionate love."
—Lauren Blakely, NY Times Bestselling Author**

\* \* \*

# Prologue

SWEAT POURED OFF Derek West's body as he manually trimmed the hedges alongside the Olympic-sized pool on the grounds of the estate where his father, Thomas, worked as the groundskeeper, his mother the maid. And where he and his family resided in the guesthouse on the edge of the property.

On such a blistering August afternoon, he'd rather be at Jones Beach with his friends, chilling out, drinking, and celebrating the dwindling days before college, but that wasn't his life. His father needed him and he was here to help.

The Storms family liked their yard elegant and perfect, and Derek's father was paid to comply. No electric hedge trimmer for him. Which meant as Derek worked under the broiling-hot sun, he could hear Cassie Storms and her friends at the pool, dishing gossip, as usual.

Cassie was his age, but she and her friends went to private school while Derek attended public. He was around enough to recognize the girls and know them by name. And he was more than interested in Cassie, especially since last night.

He'd been sitting on the porch of the guesthouse, drinking a beer long after his parents and younger sister had gone to sleep. He'd have to hide the bottle from his father, but that didn't stop him. Cassie had been out by the pool with her friends, until one by one they'd left, leaving her alone. With a little liquid courage in him, Derek had made his way over to where she sat, her shiny brown hair hanging over her shoulders, her brown eyes wide as he'd joined her.

*"Hey," he said, sitting next to her on the lounge chair.*

*"Hey." Her brows furrowed in confusion.*

*For as long as Derek had lived on the property, they'd managed to go their separate ways. He, taking a smaller driveway out to the main road, Cassie using the main entrance to the big house. But he'd always noticed her, and he'd be a liar if he didn't admit to jerking off to thoughts of the girl in the mansion many nights as he lay in his tiny room and stared at the glow of lights across the way.*

*"Want a sip?" He extended his hand, offering her the bottle.*

*She shook her head. He wasn't surprised. Cassie Storms*

2

was a good girl.

"Chicken?" he asked, goading her.

Her cheeks turned a cute pink. "No." She paused as if wrestling with herself before coming to a decision. "Fine." She grabbed the bottle from his hand and took a long drink, then wrinkled her nose.

"What's wrong?"

"It tastes a lot different than wine."

He held back a snort. Of course the rich girl drank wine.

"But I kind of liked the taste." She drew her tongue over her lips, soaking up what remained of the flavor and causing his dick to harden inside his shorts.

He handed her the beer again and she took another sip. They talked about the heat and going away to school and shared the rest of the beer. She wanted to major in business and help run her father's media company one day.

Derek? He just wanted a degree, a way out of being somebody's servant, the way his parents were. He was good at computer coding, and he figured he'd start there since it came easily to him. His father had bought him a state-of-the-art computer for Christmas, and Derek knew his dad was still paying off the expensive machine.

"I should go inside," Cassie said, but she didn't seem in any hurry to leave.

Instead she turned toward him, her thigh brushing his, their skin touching. Everything about her was soft, from her skin with a light dusting of freckles on her nose to her voice, and he was mesmerized by her. Need rushed through his body, desire for her overwhelming.

He leaned closer until their breaths mingled, malt from the beer and sweetness from her. And though her eyes opened wide, she didn't pull away. So he closed the distance and kissed her, his lips coming down on hers.

The kiss was sweet, no tongue, but it was the hottest thing Derek had experienced in forever.

"Cassie!" A female voice from the direction of her house yelled out her name.

"Oh!" She jumped back and rose to her feet. Golden flecks sparkled in her brown eyes as she stared back at him. "I have to go."

"Meet me tomorrow," he said, not ready for this—whatever this was—to end.

"But—"

"Late like tonight. Say you left something out by the pool. I'll be waiting."

She blinked and nodded. "Okay," she said in a breathy voice.

"Cassandra! It's time to come in."

Her cheeks flamed. "They treat me like a child. I can't wait to go away to school."

He knew the feeling of wanting to get away.

She turned to go.

"Tomorrow night," he reminded her, hating that he might sound desperate.

*"Okay." She nodded, her expression eager, before she swung around and ran to the big house that always seemed so far away to him.*

Derek shook his head to clear the memories of last night, knowing the bulge in his shorts couldn't be ignored. She was hot and his cock got hard just looking at her in her tiny bikini with her tits popping over the edge of the material. And earlier, her tight ass had wriggled his way when they'd risen to dip in the pool. He pressed a hand to the painful bulge in his pants.

At least the hedges and bushes covered him from the chest down. But from his position, he had a perfect view of the girls and was within earshot of their conversation.

"I'm hot," Trina Davies, a curvy blonde and Cassie's close friend, whined. "Can't you get Marie to bring us more iced tea? What are you paying her for anyway?"

Derek clenched his fists as the bitch spoke about his mother. Not even her big tits and curves were enough to make up for her attitude.

"Trina's right. If Marisol took so long, my mom would fire her ass." This from Anna Davis, the redhead of the group.

Derek glanced over the top of the bushes in time to see Cassie glance between her two friends. But she didn't say anything. Didn't defend his mother.

He'd wanted to like her, had liked her last night. But just the fact that she'd hang out with these girls told him all he needed to know about what was inside the pretty face and hot body. And Derek was less than impressed and really fucking disappointed.

He continued to watch them in silence, unnoticed.

Cassie chewed on her fingernail before finally speaking. "If Marie doesn't come out in five minutes, I'll go in and see what's keeping her."

God forbid she should pour the drinks and carry them outside herself. Poor little rich girl, he thought in disgust. What had he been thinking, asking her to meet him tonight?

Cassie pulled her hair off her neck and secured the long strands with a ponytail holder she'd been wearing around her wrist.

Without warning, Derek sneezed, calling attention to himself. He ducked down, hoping they hadn't noticed him staring.

The giggles that followed told him he'd been busted, and his face flamed hot with embarrassment.

"Did you see that? He's watching us," Anna said and not in a whisper.

"He's so hot," Trina added. "I'd totally do him," she said, loud enough to make sure he heard.

Derek wasn't sure whether to be proud or pissed at

the way they spoke about him. As if him listening didn't mean a thing.

"He's totally fuckable," Anna agreed. "But not the guy you bring home to meet your father. Isn't that right, Cass?"

Derek stiffened. This was her chance to prove she wasn't like her bitchy friends. She *knew* he was listening.

"Cass?" Trina pushed her for an answer.

"No, definitely not good enough to bring home to Daddy," she said, dutifully and as expected.

A sucker punch would have hurt less.

Fuck her. Fuck them all, Derek thought.

He couldn't wait to get the hell out of here at the end of the summer. Thank God he had the brains to get a scholarship that let him go far away from here. He'd miss his parents, but he was grateful for the chance to start fresh somewhere.

Where he wasn't the gardener's kid.

# Chapter One

ALL OF CASSIE Storms' dreams were about to come true. All the hard work for Storms Consolidated, the family multimedia company, the long hours, the fight for the right to do more than the home and gardens section, were about to reach fruition. Her father, Christopher, had called a meeting of the board of directors. The rumor mill said he would be stepping down as chairman and handing over the reins to the most qualified person. Not even Cassie knew for sure, but her gut told her the time had come for him to retire.

She sat in the boardroom, the first one to arrive, waiting for the rest of the members to take their seats and for her dad to make his announcement. She didn't know for a fact that he'd give her control. After all, her father wasn't one for personal pats on the back or to reveal his hand, but Cassie had worked harder and longer hours than anyone else.

She was the only family member on staff, her brother, Spencer, roaming Europe under the guise of getting himself together. In reality, he was carrying on with women and hanging out with other ... degenerates was too harsh a word. But if there was a mess to be made, her brother tended to make it, and her parents, her father in particular, stepped in to clean things up and sweep them under the rug.

Cassie had always been interested in the media empire started by her paternal grandfather, Alexander, a man Cassie respected and emulated. A man she missed terribly. Ten years ago, he'd been diagnosed with a rare form of cancer and had handed his company over to his only child. And Christopher hadn't been as good a businessman as Alexander had hoped. Alexander passed away long before her father's choices hurt the company, but Cassie saw. And it broke her heart.

Her grandfather had been more like a parent than her own father, caring about her goals and her choices. She'd promised him she'd work for the company he loved and do great things there, just as he would have. She was determined to keep that promise, no matter how hard her father often made it.

And he did make it tough. Christopher was old-school. He hadn't understood technology or the impact e-reading and online subscriptions would have on the business. He had no idea how to manage the sheer volume of sources from which the American public now collected its news. He had been too slow to advance with the times, and as a result, Storms Consolidated was in deep trouble.

Maybe her father now understood this and that was why he'd decided to retire. No matter the reason, Cassie already had a plan in place to reposition her beloved grandfather's company, starting with their technology magazine.

Over the last six months, she'd been creating a portfolio of interviews with high-profile men and women who had made a major impact in the tech world, slowly rebuilding the company's online presence and streaming the information on social media sites. Something her father had neglected. She hadn't gotten an interview with everyone she wanted though, because her contacts were limited, due in good part to the magazine's lack of reach.

Then the idea had come to her. She'd called *him* and requested a meeting, speaking to his assistant. To her never-ending surprise, Derek West had agreed to see her.

Her stomach fluttered at the thought of seeing him again.

She hadn't spoken to him since the kiss. Hadn't

seen him since the day he'd been working on the shrubs and had overheard her high school friends belittling his mother and mocking him.

*"He's totally fuckable," Anna agreed with Trina. "But not the guy you bring home to meet your father. Isn't that right, Cass?"*

*She internally agreed, if only because her parents were snobs. But she didn't want to admit the fact out loud. Derek was listening and she didn't want to hurt his feelings.*

*But her friends pushed.*

*And Cassie caved. "No, definitely not good enough to bring home to Daddy," she said, dutifully and as expected.*

*As she uttered the words, she nearly lost her lunch.*

She'd satisfied her bitchy friends … and hit a decent guy where it hurt.

Still, she'd gathered her courage to face him and had shown up that night as he'd asked. She'd planned to apologize. To explain, if she could, about the pressure that went along with being friends with such pushy, mean girls. To tell him more about how she couldn't wait to go to college and get away from it all, and admit she wanted to make new friends. And if he accepted her apology, she'd hoped to kiss him again.

Years later, her lips still tingled at the gentleness with which he'd touched her that day. The roughness of his lips at odds with the soft kiss.

But Derek had been MIA. He'd left her sitting alone on the lounge chair by the pool, looking over at the guesthouse, wondering if he was watching her through one of the windows.

Laughing at her embarrassment.

She'd deserve it if he had been. Eventually she'd stood, and with one last look at where he lived, she'd walked back inside the house.

A few days later, she'd left for college. She made new friends, nicer girls she felt comfortable with and who made her feel like she fit in. Not people she was stuck with just because they were part of her family's social circle. She lost touch with Trina and Anna and the others, barely sparing them a thought over the years. Good riddance, she'd believed, on the rare times when they'd crossed her mind.

And over the years, she'd watched Derek West's sudden, meteoric rise in the tech world, along with his partners, Lucas Monroe and Kaden Barnes. All three were co-creators of Blink, the social media app that had taken the world by storm. She didn't miss the irony that they'd ended up in the same arena, Cassie focusing on the online tech magazine of Storms Consolidated.

An interview with the most behind-the-scenes partner of Blink would help revitalize the magazine and put them back on the map. She intended to request one.

The sound of footsteps and voices startled Cassie out of her musings. She rose to her feet as the board members walked into the room.

She shook hands with the men and women she'd known most of her life and exchanged small talk as she waited for her father to arrive.

Even this boardroom held good memories for her as a child. Not with her father, he was hardly the doting parent, but with her grandfather. Alexander would often bring her to work with him and let her sit beside him at the head of the table. He'd used a gavel to call meetings to order, and he'd bought her a mini duplicate one so she could emulate him. Even then, she'd known what she wanted to do when she grew up.

Today she would finally have her chance.

Once everyone had filled the room, her father entered, and after he, too, said his hellos, they took their seats. As her dad began to talk about his love for the company, her heart began to race with hope and excitement.

"The time has come for me to step down. My wife deserves more time than I'm able to give her while running this company."

Cassie smiled. For all her parents' faults when it came to enabling her brother and treating her, the girl, as less than, they did set an example as a couple who truly loved one another. Daniella often mentioned her desire to travel, and maybe this was her father acceding to her mother's wishes at last.

Her father cleared his throat and continued. "You all know we recently had an offer to buy Storms Consolidated that we turned down. This company was started by my father, and I intend to keep it in the family."

Hidden by the table, Cassie clenched her hands together in her lap, her pulse pounding. Even the board members murmured amongst themselves, some casting furtive glances her way. She wouldn't let them down.

Christopher expounded more on the importance of the family business, never once mentioning Cassie by name. She swallowed hard but knew he had a flair for the dramatic. And he was building up to his announcement, after all.

But the longer he spoke, the more her unease grew, and she didn't know why. Except for the fact that she was sitting *right here*. And he hadn't once looked her way or met her gaze.

"So I announce my replacement with the hopes you will give him the support and respect you've always accorded me."

*Him?* Who? Cassie's stomach churned and twisted

painfully.

"I'm excited to welcome my son, Spencer, home from Europe. He's excited and ready to tackle all the growth and changes sure to come." Christopher gestured to the door and began clapping as Cassie's brother walked into the room.

Spencer, looking tan from his time abroad, stepped up and said a few brief words, but nothing that happened next registered.

Blindsided. Devastated. Hurt. Every one of those words described her after the stunt her father had just pulled. And the sad thing was, he didn't even know it. When it came to Spencer, her father saw potential if only he helped him. And because Christopher was old-school, if his choice was between his daughter and his son, the male heir won out. Cassie's qualifications, her dedication, her drive … none of it mattered.

The day, which had started with such promise, took a nosedive, and she decided she had no desire to sit around and pretend she was happy about their new chairman who understood squat about running his own life, let alone a multimedia company. So as the board members rose from their seats to shake Spencer's hand, Cassie stood, and not meeting anyone's gaze, she walked out the door.

THE ARK WAS a bar not far from the office. She called her best friend, Amanda, to meet her after work for some good old-fashioned commiseration. In a few days, she'd have to pull herself together for the meeting with Derek West, but right now she was all about wallowing in her misery.

The bar was filled with people who came by on their way home from the office, but Cassie had arrived early and snagged a high table and chairs. She always kept a casual set of clothes at the office, and she'd changed before heading out. Since Amanda worked in an easygoing ad agency, she was dressed similarly in jeans and a long-sleeve tee shirt when she arrived.

"I got here as soon as I could," Amanda said, sliding into the tall chair and hanging her purse over the side closest to the wall.

"I appreciate it. What do you want?" Cassie asked as she signaled for a busy waitress. "I waited for you, and now I'm beyond ready for a drink."

"A white wine spritzer," Amanda said to the woman who walked over.

"A whiskey on the rocks for me, and please put both on my tab." She waved away Amanda's open-mouthed, obvious objection. She'd needed this meeting. The least she could do was treat.

"That bad a day you need hard liquor?" Amanda asked, tucking a strand of her blonde hair behind her ear.

"Worse."

Cassie's grandfather had introduced her to whiskey when she'd turned twenty. No, she hadn't been legal, but he had been dying. And as he'd explained, she needed to learn to drink with the men if she was going to hold her own. At the time, Cassie thought he was being ridiculous, but over the years, sharing a whiskey with the board members had enabled them to look at her as less delicate and more as one of them. Ridiculous but true.

Today she felt like she needed something strong—to remind her she was tough despite what had occurred earlier.

"So spill. I'm here. What happened? Last time we spoke, you were flying high."

"Yes, well, that's the problem with assumptions."

The waitress delivered their drinks, and Cassie waited until she could take a long sip and feel the burn down her chest before she said the words out loud.

"My father turned everything over to Spencer."

Amanda blinked. "It's not April Fools."

"And I'm not joking."

"What. The. Fuck?" Amanda had known Cassie since they'd met abroad, in Prague, during their junior year of college. They'd gotten close and stayed friends through business school for Cassie and Amanda working her way up in advertising. She was from the Midwest, and she'd come home with Cassie for some holidays, which meant she'd met Spencer.

Had been hit on by Spencer. Had seen her brother in action more than once. In other words, her reaction was justified by experience.

"My father started to expound on Storms Consolidated being a family business, and how important it was to keep it in the *family*, and I was so sure—" Cassie's voice caught unexpectedly, and she ducked her head, hating the emotional reaction to the announcement.

Amanda reached across the table and squeezed her hand. "It's a minor setback. Your brother will screw up in no time, and the company will be yours."

"Not how I want to get it. I earned my place. Spencer hasn't worked a day in his life. I'll be lucky if there's a company left when Spencer's done running it. What was my father thinking?" Cassie finished the drink, knowing that one glass was all she was up to tonight.

"Listen to me. You can still carry on with your plan to bring the company into this century. You can work around your brother and ... I don't know. Outlast him."

"Well, I definitely intend to take the meeting with Derek West and continue the upward trend with the tech side."

"Good." Amanda eyed her with concern. "Are you okay?"

Cassie swallowed hard. "I will be. I have no choice."

"You're up to the meeting with your hot billionaire?" Amanda asked.

"He's not my billionaire." Even if he was hot.

She'd seen pictures of him, recent photos, and the boy she'd known had more than filled out. He was now a sexy, self-confident man.

But she appreciated her friend's attempt to lighten the mood. Unfortunately, this subject wasn't any easier. "I told you about our history. I can't imagine why he agreed to see me now."

"Your reputation precedes you? I'm sure he assumes you want an interview, and he knows you'll do a kick-ass job."

That was one way to look at it. Or … "Maybe he figures it's time to make me pay."

Amanda rolled her eyes. "Now who's being dramatic?"

Cassie shivered and ran her hands up and down her arms. "I guess I'll find out soon enough." Either the week would take a more positive turn or she'd end up feeling even lower than she already was.

DEREK WEST LISTENED to his assistant run through his appointments for the day, but his mind wasn't on anything but his ten a.m.

Cassie Storms.

He'd been shocked when Becky told him she'd called and asked to meet. Derek had thought of her over the years for many reasons, none of them good. The Storms family was responsible for a shit ton of pain and heartache for Derek's parents, both his father who had passed away, and his mother. Derek had never forgotten.

And Cassie, well, she'd set the bar for how he viewed rich girls for most of his life. Which made dating complicated since he'd become wealthy himself. It was hard to be himself around women. He didn't believe that they didn't want him for his money, and if they were well off, he immediately had his guard up, distrusting what kind of bitchy personality lay beneath the façade they presented to the world.

Cassie couldn't have been sweeter the night he'd kissed her, but she'd had no problem humiliating him in front of her friends the very next day. His cheeks still burned with mortification when he thought of it.

He hadn't shown up that night as planned, and he hadn't expected her to be there either. Curiosity had him watching from his bedroom window though, and she had waited for him out by the pool. He couldn't imagine why, nor did he care. He'd gotten some small consolation knowing she was waiting in vain, maybe feeling an ounce of the humiliation she'd dished out to him.

As he'd watched her shoulders slump and she seemed to curl in on herself, a part of him had felt bad. Until he'd remembered her friends' laughter at their cruel comments about him being fuckable but not good enough to take home to their fathers.

Bitches. He'd turned away from the window and never looked back.

He'd left for college a few days later, where life had changed. He'd busted his ass on his scholarship and worked jobs to have money to live. But while there, he'd met Kade and Luke, his best friends, his brothers.

And they'd developed Blink. His life had taken a one-hundred-and-eighty-degree turn from his poor roots. He'd been too late to help his father, but he'd been able to improve his mother's life. He just couldn't bring his father back. Too little, too late, for which he blamed the Storms family.

These days, Derek considered himself as much an entrepreneur as a technology guru, and he often purchased failing businesses with the goal of either setting them back on their feet or dismantling them and selling off the pieces. Either option worked, whichever made him the most money. So when he'd heard that Storms Consolidated was in trouble, he'd set his sights on acquiring it and put in a generous offer under a shell company name.

No way would Christopher Storms ever sell his beloved company to his ex-gardener's son. A man he'd fired after accusing his wife of stealing family jewelry. The son of a woman he'd had arrested. A family he'd turned on after they'd given him years of service, leaving them with no references, no place to live, and no health insurance. The latter was something Derek would never forgive him for.

Needless to say, he didn't want to buy the company in order to right the ship. He wanted to run it into the ground and destroy anything with the name Storms. But even with Derek's name hidden, Christopher Storms had turned down the offer.

That was fine. Derek had tried to acquire the thing on a lark. A shot at taking the man down, but Derek wasn't ruled by revenge. If the opportunity came again, he'd give it another chance, but he'd moved on. And then he'd heard from Cassie.

In the last year, her name started turning up on some damn fine articles on people who ran in Derek's world. He wasn't stupid. He figured she wanted to interview him. Many had tried, but he rarely granted access because he didn't want anyone digging into his family or his past. He was a private man.

He'd agreed to meet with Cassie out of curiosity. What kind of woman had she become? How far would she go to get what she wanted? Would she beg? He knew the company wasn't doing well, and an interview with him would be a coup nobody else had succeeded in obtaining. He wouldn't mind seeing her grovel before he said no.

Petty? Maybe. Definitely. But he'd looked her up on social media and was still intrigued enough by the woman to want to see her one more time.

"Derek, you haven't heard a word I said," Becky chided. They ran a casual office, first names, jeans and tee-shirts, except for Kade's wife, who, when she was in the office as his assistant, liked to dress up.

He shook his head, knowing Becky was right. His head was elsewhere. "Sorry, I have a lot on my mind. But I have a ten o'clock appointment, Cassandra Storms?"

"Yes."

"Please have her wait exactly ten minutes before sending her in." No reason to see her immediately.

Let her sweat before they faced each other again.

Ironically he was the one who sweat when Becky announced Cassie had arrived and he counted down the minutes until ten after the hour. The time ticked past slowly.

He glanced at his watch. Finally he could get this

show going, he thought and rang for Becky to send Cassie in.

He pushed himself to his feet just as she stepped into his office. He thought he was prepared, but online photos and social media profiles hadn't done her justice. She'd filled out, her curves more that of a woman than a young girl. Her long brown hair was thick, made for him to wrap around his hand as he tugged her head back and had his way with her, kissing her everywhere.

She was fucking hot. Sexy and alluring in a way she hadn't been when she was eighteen. And he was just as attracted to her now as he'd been then. More so, even. That was something for which he hadn't been prepared.

"Mr. West, thank you for agreeing to see me," she said in a slightly deeper voice than he remembered.

"Ms. Storms." He strode out from behind his desk to greet her, extending his hand.

She slid her palm against his, her skin soft and silky, much like he imagined the rest of her would be.

Shit.

He needed to maintain control. *Be* in control. "I admit I was curious why you'd contact me after all these years,"

"Well, I…" She trailed off, obviously gathering her thoughts. She curled her hands around her clutch purse, showing more nerves than he thought she'd want him to see.

He took pity on her and gestured to the chairs across from his desk. "Have a seat," he said and waited for her to settle in.

She crossed her legs at the ankles and waited. So prim and proper. Such a lady, which only made him want to see her messed up, from his hands in her hair, his mouth on hers.

He cupped the back of his neck, realizing he'd clearly underestimated her impact. Too bad he knew what lay beneath the cool façade. But he couldn't tear his gaze from her trembling hands, a nervous gesture that didn't jibe with the self-confident bitch he thought she'd be.

If she wasn't ready to get to the point of this meeting, he was. "I take it you're interested in me?" he asked.

Her cheeks flushed at his not-so-subtle innuendo. "Very," she replied, not missing a beat, her lips lifting in an amused smile.

And in that second, they were thinking the same thing. He wanted to back her into the wall and kiss her senseless, and from the way her lips parted and a soft breath of air expelled from her lips, she felt the same. The chemistry between them was still strong.

She drew a deep breath and let it out slowly. "Actually, I thought you might be interested in letting me do a piece about you for *Take a Byte*," she said of her online tech magazine.

He nodded slowly. "I suspected as much. And the truth is, ever since the IPO and Kade's stint on morning television, I've had pressure to do interviews and reveal more about myself. I've read your articles on Zuckerberg and Spiegel. You do your research and you're a fair reporter," he said.

She was a talented writer and interviewer. Their awkward past couldn't diminish that fact.

Her eyes opened wide in surprise. "Thank you."

"I'm just telling you the truth."

Her cheeks flushed with pride. "I've worked hard to make us relevant again," she murmured.

"And you've done a great job."

"So you'll let me interview you?" she asked, leaning forward in her seat, her blouse parting, revealing the enticing swell of her breasts.

His throat went dry. "Unfortunately, no. I don't do interviews," he said in a rough voice.

Instead of her shoulders deflating, she sat up straighter, her determination coming through. "I wish you'd reconsider. I can give it any slant you like. As far as the world is concerned, you're an enigma. Any coverage will bring in readers."

He shook his head. Derek was all about protecting

his family, and refusing interviews accomplished that. He didn't think Cassie would be any more interested in digging into his humble beginnings than he was in disclosing them. Not when it meant revealing that her parents had been his parents' employers.

The story was ugly for both of them, as he assumed she knew, and he doubted she'd want her parents' names dragged into the article by revisiting the past. And though he knew he could get her to focus on his successes, once she published her piece, it was only a matter of time before another journalist dug deeper and discovered more. His father had been through enough.

"I'm sorry but I can't."

She rose to her feet and met his gaze head on. "So why agree to see me? Did you want to humiliate me in exchange for what I did to you when we were younger?"

"What? No. That wasn't it at all."

Her shoulders rolled inward. "I wouldn't blame you any more than I blame you for not wanting to do an interview with me … but there is something I want to say before I go."

He raised an eyebrow and waited.

"I'm sorry," she blurted out.

He shook his head, certain he'd heard wrong. "Excuse me?"

"I'm sorry for what I said all those years ago." Her cheeks burned not with embarrassment but shame.

He saw the regret in her eyes, and he could not have been more surprised.

She twisted her hands anxiously in front of her. "I have no excuse except that I was young and susceptible to peer pressure. I didn't mean what I said."

"Didn't you?" His voice came out harsher than he'd intended, and she flinched at his angry tone.

"What?" she asked.

"Didn't you mean what you said? Or are you saying you would have been happy to take me home to your father?"

Her throat moved up and down. "No. He wouldn't approve. But I never should have said as much in front of you. And you can believe me or not, but I am sorry. I've regretted that day for years."

He softened toward her for the first time.

She shifted and picked her purse up from the floor by her chair. "I see now why the interview is a bad idea. Thank you for hearing me out." She started for the door, her chin held high.

He reached out and grabbed her arm. "Cassie, wait," he said, suddenly struggling between letting go of the anger toward the girl she'd been in the past and forgiving the woman she was now. That woman called to him on a primal, baser level. As a man, he wanted her.

She turned slowly and glanced down at where his hand remained. "We're back on first names now?"

Her skin was so soft beneath his fingers, and he immediately released her. "We are. And I accept your apology."

Because her admission humbled her and showed him a side he hadn't anticipated existed. It gave him pause. Made him want to know more about this enigmatic woman who vacillated between discomfort and calm, embarrassment and confidence.

"Have dinner with me on Friday," he said, the words tumbling out before he could think them through.

"I don't think so," she said, glancing down, not meeting his gaze.

"Why not?" He leaned forward, forcing her to glance up. "You can use the time to try and convince me to change my mind." He was intrigued by her, her honesty he'd never seen coming. And he desired her too.

"Why the sudden change of heart?"

"You pique my interest," he said honestly. "So what do you say?"

She sighed, a smile pulling at her full, sexy lips. "You're persistent."

"I can be ... when I want something." And he realized, despite the years that had passed, he still wanted her.

"Fine. We can have dinner. I'd be a fool to walk away from the opportunity to do my best ... convincing."

# Chapter Two

N OT LONG AFTER leaving Derek's office, Cassie was summoned to her father's house for a meeting. Never a good sign and especially not now, with her brother home and in charge of the business. As she traveled back to her parents' place on the train, she couldn't focus on what awaited her.

Her head was still spinning from meeting with Derek for the first time in years. She couldn't believe he was so impressed with her skills. Even though he'd declined the interview, his compliment had been the highlight of a really shitty week, as was the fact that he was giving her another chance to convince him to change his mind. But her thoughts weren't on how much the interview would benefit *Take a Byte* and help give their online views and presence a much-needed boost.

No, she couldn't stop thinking about what Derek

looked like now. His blue eyes were still crystal and clear, his face handsome and more mature. No longer a lanky teen, he was muscular in all the right places. His forearms were bulky, as was his chest, all clearly from working out. And since he wore a long-sleeve shirt with the sleeves pushed up, his sexy tattoos were clearly visible. If his chiseled features and good looks weren't enough, he smelled delicious too.

Derek West was a sexy, imposing man, and she was extremely attracted to him. So much so that she'd had inappropriate thoughts of wrapping herself around him and breathing him in, all the while feeling all those hard muscles against her softer ones. It had been a long time since she'd been in a relationship, and she wasn't interested in one-night stands, but her deprived body had responded to Derek West.

By the time the cab arrived at her parents' house, she'd pulled her mind back to what her father might want. She paid the driver and headed up the walk. The weather was cold, and she pulled her jacket tighter around her, a barrier against the winter wind.

She knocked on the front door and Greta, their current housekeeper, let her in.

"Miss Cassie, your father and brother are in the study," she said, taking Cassie's jacket the minute she shrugged it off her shoulders.

She thought of Derek's parents and realized she

hadn't asked how they were. Cassie had come home from college during a freshman year visit to find the family had moved out of the guest home. They found another job, her father had said, and refused to discuss *the help* any further. Cassie had been sad because she'd liked Derek's mom when she'd worked for them over the years. Her parents no longer had live-in help. After Derek's mother, they'd begun to use a service that provided bonded housekeepers.

Cassie cleaned her own place and allowed her mother to send someone in once a week for deeper cleaning. She wasn't the snob her parents were, and appreciated the fact that she earned enough to cover the cost. She knew she was born into a lucky lot in life, no matter how frustrating her family might be.

Speaking of … she walked into her father's study. Christopher and Spencer were looking at something on the big-screen computer. Neither glanced up as she entered, so she cleared her throat, announcing her presence.

"Cassandra, it's about time you got here," her father said impatiently.

"Hi, sis."

She forced a smile at them both. "I was in the city." She refused to elaborate or give either of them any information about her plans for the magazine.

Her brother might be running things, but he didn't

need to know her intentions. Until she knew if they were on the same page for the direction of the business, she'd keep her strategies to herself.

"I'm here now. What did you want to discuss?"

"The guesthouse," her father said, taking her off guard. "You've been living there for a while, and now with Spencer home, I think it's only fair that he be able to move in."

"Wait. You're kicking me out of my house?"

Since returning from grad school, she'd been living in the guesthouse, where Derek's family once resided. Cassie paid rent, just as she'd do anywhere else. When she'd first moved back, she hadn't wanted to live in Manhattan. The commute to the city wasn't terrible from Long Island, and she loved the home she'd made for herself there. She certainly had never expected to be *evicted* in favor of her sibling.

Spencer walked over and slung an arm over her shoulder. "Dad thought it would be good for me to live close to him while I'm getting my footing running things. You can move back into the house. No problem."

She spun away from him and glared. "Why don't you live at home if it's no problem?" she asked.

Her father pinned her with his steady gaze. "A man needs his space and his privacy. Surely you understand."

She stared at them, more betrayal settling in her stomach. "I'm not moving back in with my parents. I'll find a place in the city."

"You see? I told you she'd be reasonable," her father said, as if he'd given her a choice.

"Is there anything else?" she asked, eager to get away from them both.

"No. We have work to do," Spencer said, dismissing her.

Cassie walked out of the office, and it took all her self-control not to slam the door behind her. It would serve them right if she took a job with a rival company, except then she wouldn't be working to save what her grandfather had founded. She wouldn't let the two male chauvinists drive her off. She'd stay and pull her weight, knowing she was accomplishing her personal goals if nothing else.

If she couldn't run Storms Consolidated and fix the mess her father had made, at the very least she could make *Take a Byte* a site people turned to first for technology information and updates. Something Alexander would be proud of.

First, however, she needed to find a new place to live. She made it as far as the front door when her mother called out her name.

"Cassandra, come talk to me before you go."

She blew out a deep breath. "Did you know they're

kicking me out of the guesthouse?"

Her mother, dressed in a pair of black wool slacks and a silk blouse, clasped her hands in front of her and nodded. She tucked a strand of her brown, bobbed hair behind her ear. "That's why I want you to come talk." She shot Cassie a beseeching look.

Betrayal sat deep in her stomach, but she decided to hear Daniella out. Cassie followed her mother into the kitchen and waited while she made them each a cup of tea, then settled into a seat at the table.

"I know you don't understand your father," her mother began.

"No, I understand him. What Spencer wants, Spencer gets. If I didn't have such strong feelings for Grandpa and the company, I'd be long gone," Cassie said, ignoring the steaming-hot tea.

"Honey, your father is complicated. Part of the problem is that he's old-fashioned. His son is a reflection of him, and he's going to do what he can to make him happy and keep him on the straight and narrow."

Cassie swallowed hard. "At my expense. Look, it's not that I don't understand him protecting Spencer, I do. But handing over the company I've put my heart and soul into? Asking me to move out of my home?"

Her mother placed a hand on Cassie's. "I disagree with what he's doing, but I want you to know why I think he does it."

"You just said it's because Spencer is a reflection of him."

"Partly. The other part is because he knows you can stand on your own. You're going to come out on top no matter what. You always succeed at what you do. It's why I'm so proud of you."

"Those are your feelings, Mom, not his."

Her mother squeezed her hand, and a lump formed in Cassie's throat.

This was how things had always been. Her father would do something or miss an event, and her mother would make an excuse for the man. Daniella loved him, but Cassie would never understand or forgive how he treated her.

Daniella's words didn't take away the sting or the pain, but Cassie was resilient. Her mother was right. She'd pull it together and land on her feet.

DEREK DIDN'T PLAN on letting Cassie convince him to do the interview. He did, however, decide to go all out for their dinner. The hard truth was, he wanted to impress her. He needed her to see him as the successful man he'd become, not the wannabe son of the help. And if he could coax her into his bed so he could satisfy his desire for her, that would be a win, too.

He booked a private room in an exclusive restaurant that would normally take months to get a regular reservation. He called her himself to confirm their Friday night date, not wanting to keep it impersonal with Becky being the go-between.

And though he didn't know Cassie well enough to judge, her voice sounded like she was feeling down. For a brief moment, he wondered if she'd cancel, but she didn't. So he offered to pick her up, not caring that she lived on Long Island and he'd be going out of his way only to have to drive back into Manhattan. She'd insisted on meeting him at the restaurant.

His father had raised him to be a gentleman, and it didn't sit right with him not to drive her. But she wouldn't give in, and so he waited at the front of the restaurant, determined to join her when she arrived.

He caught sight of her getting out of a taxi right on time. He shook his head, still not pleased that he wasn't in charge, paying for the cab.

His visceral reaction to seeing her again caught him off guard. Her hair was free, flowing over her shoulders, her makeup done up more than the last time, and from the long legs peeking out from beneath her wool coat, she wore a dress that, with his luck, would have him drooling all through dinner. His heart began to pound in his chest, and a fresh wave of desire hit him hard.

Hoping she couldn't see or notice his body's response, he stepped into the chilly air and met her on the sidewalk. "You made it," he said by way of greeting.

She inclined her head and smiled, her gaze traveling over him appreciatively. "I said I would. And now I'm glad I did."

"Let's get out of the cold." He placed a hand at the small of her back and led her toward the restaurant, holding the door open for her to walk inside.

She removed her jacket, revealing a white cashmere dress, the slight dip in the front showing her slender neck, the slight swell of her breasts, and a thin gold chain. No heavy jewelry in sight.

"You look beautiful," he said, the words out before he could think them through.

Her eyes swung to his. "Thank you," she said, clearly surprised by the compliment.

They obviously had a long way to go before they were comfortable around each other, but he was working on it. If he thought he'd wanted her before, he was even more certain now. Getting her out of his system would be the healthy thing to do.

"Come. I reserved a private room in the back," he said.

"Derek! You didn't have to do that," she murmured, sounding pleased that he had.

He liked the sound of his name on her lips. Would

love to hear it when his cock was deep inside her warm, wet body, he thought, clenching his hand into a tight fist.

Emotional comfort might be far away, but physical attraction was here and strong, he thought, acknowledging that he was powerless to fight her pull.

They sat in a rounded booth, side by side, his thigh close to hers. His dick was hard, and he was grateful for the cover of the table.

A waiter came to take their order—steak au poivre for both of them, baked potatoes, hers loaded with sour cream, and creamed spinach. He grinned at that. A girl after his own heart. Not a light salad eater, he thought, pleased.

He glanced at the wine menu and ordered a bottle of Miner Cabernet, a red wine to go with the meal. "I'm assuming that's okay? If you still like wine, that is?" he asked before the waiter took his leave.

Her lips lifted in a knowing grin. She remembered too. "I still prefer it to beer. Though once in a while, sharing a bottle can be fun."

Her joking words about their shared past broke the ice, and he relaxed, knowing she was feeling more comfortable with him.

The waiter tilted his head and excused himself, pulling the door closed behind him, but he returned quickly and poured their wine, pausing for the ritual tasting. Finally, though, they were alone again.

"Well," she said into the silence.

"Well." He raised his glass. "To ... renewed acquaintances."

She smiled and raised her glass before taking a sip. "Delicious," she murmured. "You have good taste."

"I learned," he admitted, leaning in closer. "So tell me, how have you been? It really has been a long time."

She nodded. "I'm good," she said, her voice dipping, reminiscent of what he'd heard in her tone over the phone. Then she grew silent.

"I don't know you well ... or at all, but I'm pretty sure there's something going on and you're not okay."

"Are you a mind reader?" she asked teasingly, but the dimming light in her eyes gave her away.

"No, but it's twice now I've heard something in your tone that tells me you're upset."

A muscle ticked in her jaw. "You're right."

"I'm listening ... if you want to talk." And he hoped she did. His curiosity about her was rampant.

He leaned back, placing one arm behind her back, his fingertips grazing the soft fuzz of her dress on her shoulder. Her gaze flew to his, but she didn't shift or move away.

"Okay, well, where to begin?" She steepled her fingers and peered over at him. "Things at *Take a Byte* are going well for me, but I can't say the same for Storms Consolidated. My father is retiring, and I thought he'd name me as his successor."

During Derek's attempt at acquiring the company, he'd heard rumblings of problems with the bottom line, a few firings to accommodate cost cutting. He hadn't, however, known the chairman was planning on retiring.

"He didn't choose you?"

"No." She turned toward him, her gaze meeting his. "He decided my brother, who has been traveling Europe for the last year, deserves the job over me. I've worked there since college, I've proven my loyalty and my ability, and yet being a man holds more weight."

Damn, that had to hurt. "I'm sorry."

"It gets worse."

He raised an eyebrow, wondering how.

"I've been evicted by my own family," she said, lifting the glass and taking a long sip of wine.

"Seriously?" he asked, joining her for a drink.

She nodded. "I ... um ... I've been staying in the guesthouse, where you used to live." She glanced down, aware of the awkwardness she'd injected into the conversation.

No wonder she hadn't wanted him to pick her up tonight, he thought, stiffening at the reminder of their pasts, the status differences between them growing up.

Of her father's role in hurting his family.

But, he reminded himself, he'd known these things going in. If he was going to spend any time with Cassie, for whatever reason, even if it involved his dick, he was going to have to deal with the facts. And not be put off every time she mentioned something that brought up past pain.

"What do you mean you were evicted?" he asked, focusing on the conversation.

"My father asked me to move out so my brother could move in. A man needs his space," she said in a mocking imitation of her parent.

"Are you kidding me?" What kind of father threw his own child out? Derek's family looked out for each other. His mom didn't play favorites between Derek and his sister, Brenda, nor would she hurt one in favor of the other.

"I'm completely serious." She raised one shoulder in a delicate shrug. "I've had the rug ripped out from under me. Twice."

"That sucks," he said, feeling sorry for her, something he doubted she would appreciate.

She laughed. "That's an understatement. But I'm not giving up," she said, squaring her shoulders. "The company means as much to me now as it did when I was younger. More so. Before my grandfather died, I promised him I would do great things at his company, and I'm determined to fix what my father let go wrong. I want to make my grandfather proud," she said, her voice thick.

Derek knew what it was like to make a promise to a sick person you loved. Studying the set of her jaw, the stubborn lift of her chin, he admired her for not falling apart when other women might crumble.

"I'm going to right the ship despite losing out to my brother," she said, a determined glint in her eye.

There was something inherently sexy about her commitment. And though he despised her father, he liked what he was learning about Cassie. She was nothing like the spoiled brat he'd decided she was all those years ago.

In fact, she was similar to the girl he'd pegged her for initially. And his gut was usually right.

"How do you plan to fix things?" he asked, genuinely curious.

"I'm going to start by making *Take a Byte* a force to be reckoned with."

"Then interview me. That'll give you a leg up on any of the competition," he said, shocked when the words came out of his mouth.

He hadn't planned to give in, and she hadn't yet asked him to. He was offering. Helping her succeed would be a fuck you to the man who didn't believe in her. The same man who'd screwed his family over. It didn't hurt that Derek wanted to sleep with her and he'd just given himself a reason to spend more time with her.

"And here I was waiting for dessert to ask," she said, laughing. "Derek, thank you. Are you sure?"

"We can work something out," he said, uncomfortable with the idea but willing to give up his privacy for the cause.

"As for a place to live, what are you looking for? A rental or something to buy?"

"A rental. I think I should see if I like living in the city before I commit to anything permanent there."

He could help her there too.

"I own a few buildings with empty apartments for rent. I'm not sure what your budget is, but you can take a look and decide."

Her eyes opened wide with delight. "Really? Because I've been completely overwhelmed. I'm not sure where I'd want to live or how to begin to look. I was going to call a Realtor, but I'd rather take the word of someone I know than do a full-blown search. Something tells me my brother will want me out ... oh, yesterday."

She frowned and he wanted to kiss the scowl off her pretty face. Before he could react to that thought, she leaned over, placed her arms around his neck, and hugged him tight.

"Thank you. You've turned around an otherwise awful week."

She took him off guard, even more so when her full breasts pressed against his chest and he inhaled the fragrant, delicious scent of her hair. His dick stood at alert, desire taking hold.

She tilted her head back, her gaze meeting his. Her lips parted and his heart rate sped up, awareness pulsing through his veins. He raised his hand, cupping the back of her neck in his palm, pulling her closer to him, their mouths millimeters apart.

Teasing him.

Testing him.

He failed and sealed his lips over hers.

Similar to years ago, the kiss was soft, gentle, but now he was a man who knew what he wanted, and the desire to really taste her overwhelmed him. He slid his tongue across her lower lip, eliciting a soft moan that undid him, and his tongue stole past her lips, tangling with hers. He tightened his grip on the back of her neck and lost himself in the warmth of her mouth, the seduction of her kiss.

Time stood still. Their lips melded; his mind focused on the delicious taste of her and the feel of her tongue twined with his. Until the sound of the door opening jarred him back to reality.

She jerked back. He immediately released his hold

and met her gaze, unable to stop the smile when he saw her damp lips.

A quick glance down revealed her nipples had beaded into tight points, in complete agreement with his thick erection, tenting his slacks.

The waiter mumbled his apology and began to serve dinner. While he worked, Derek held her gaze, sensual awareness reciprocated in her eyes while a deep flush stained her cheeks. But she didn't look away.

When the waiter finally departed, Derek cleared his throat and raised his glass, taking a long sip of wine.

"That was ... unexpected," she murmured.

"I'd call it extremely expected. From the first time we met as kids to now. The attraction's been there."

"Agreed." She wrapped a hand around the stem of her glass. "But attraction aside, I have another question. You agreed to the interview. Offered to help me find a place to live. Not to be rude, but why are you being so nice to me?" she asked.

Attraction aside, she'd asked a good question. One for which he had no answer. When tonight was over, he was going to have to take his temperature and figure out what the fuck was wrong with him, that he was rolling over for this woman without her asking for anything in return.

Or maybe that was the reason. She didn't ask. She

was unassuming and sweet, neither of which he'd expected. Not to mention, he wanted her. Badly. The businessman in him recognized that in getting closer, she might also provide him with insight into the company he hadn't given up on acquiring. That was an bonus.

He raised one shoulder. "I suppose it's as simple as you need something and I have the ability to help, that's all," he said, giving her the simplest answer. One even he could live with. For now.

"Well, thank you again." A big smile covered her face.

"You're welcome."

With the kiss behind them but never out of his mind, they spent the rest of the evening with small talk, but eventually the night ended.

He hailed her a cab and waited alongside her on the sidewalk. They'd already exchanged phone numbers to arrange for her to see apartments over the weekend. He'd have to get in touch with his property manager and get the unit numbers and keys, but that was no problem.

A cab pulled to a stop and Derek opened the door. He slid an arm around her back and pulled her toward him, his gaze meeting hers. "Thanks for having dinner with me," he said in a gruff voice.

"Thank you for forgiving me." Her face flushed

red that had nothing to do with the winter chill.

Before he could reply, she brushed a kiss over his cheek, turned, and slid into the cab, leaving him aching with desire. And confounded by how she'd defied all his expectations and, in the process, had him going against all his own good intentions.

All because he liked and desired her.

But Cassie wasn't a one-night-stand kind of woman, and he'd be spending time with her, both helping and getting to know her better, before inevitably falling into bed with the woman he'd once considered his enemy.

As long as he reminded himself that sex was all there could be between them.

She was still Cassie *Storms*, after all.

# Chapter Three

C ASSIE SAT AT her desk, her mind on the article she intended to write about Derek. Before Friday night, she'd known nothing about him, had no gut instinct on how to slant the piece. Now she did. Derek West was a decent guy. In fact, she'd been completely caught off guard by how kind he'd been to her.

Not only had he accepted her apology but he'd offered her the two things she needed most. The interview—something he disdained, yet was willing to do for her—and help finding a place to live. She'd go so far as to say they'd put the past behind them as much as possible. She didn't kid herself. There had been—and would be again—more awkward moments between them. Like when she'd admitted to living in the house he'd grown up in.

She'd seen the wariness go up, the defensive posture and a brief flare of what looked like anger in his eyes before he'd composed himself again. She wasn't certain where that irritation stemmed from or if she'd even read him correctly, the emotion gone too quickly for her to judge.

But none of those things had anything to do with chemistry, and she and Derek had that in high doses. All she'd had to do was look at him when she arrived and unexpected desire had engulfed her quickly. And when she'd hugged him in gratitude, he'd smelled so masculine and good; her breasts had crushed against his hard chest, her nipples hardening in reaction.

She hadn't planned or expected the kiss. He knew how to take charge, and the way he'd kissed her reflected the alpha-driven man he'd become. With his hand behind her head and the hard press of his lips, she'd been lost. At least until they were interrupted by the waiter. She ran her tongue over her lips, imagining she could still taste him, before she forced her mind back to the business at hand.

Moving forward on the interview.

She called his cell phone, and he answered on the first ring. "Good morning," he said, sounding happy to hear from her.

She wondered if that good feeling would continue after he heard her idea.

"Morning. Do you have a minute? I'd like to run something by you," she said, doodling on a piece of paper on her desk as she spoke.

"For you I'll make time."

Her body warmed at his words. "I wanted to discuss the interview." And before he could change his mind, she continued. "With everyone else, I've met with them once, maybe twice, and written based on that discussion and prior research. I wanted to go in a different direction with you."

"Uh oh."

She laughed at his response. Little did he know...

"What did you have in mind?" he asked.

"I thought I could shadow you. Sort of a day in the life except over the course of a longer period of time. That way I'd get a broader perspective of what you do, how you think ... how you became the success that you are." She bit down on her bottom lip and waited for a reply.

"You do realize you're asking a lot. I don't want to open myself up for public scrutiny."

"I understand and I can give it that slant. I promise I'll respect your boundaries." She could almost hear him thinking and she held her breath.

"I'll do it for one reason," he said at last. "So I can spend more time with you."

"You won't regret it," she promised as her heart skipped a beat at his answer, equal parts thrilled for her interview and for herself personally.

Because she wanted to spend more time with him too.

DEREK WAITED FOR his partners at the gym for their Thursday night boxing, sparring and workout. He'd arrived first and ran on the treadmill for fifteen minutes before he saw Kade make his way in.

"Sorry I'm late," the other man said as he joined Derek, putting his duffel on the wooden bench by the treadmill.

"I'm here," Lucas muttered a few minutes later, jogging in, out of breath.

"Held up at work?" Derek asked neither man in particular. He stepped off the machine and wiped his face down with a towel.

"No, Lexie baked some chocolate chip cookies, which are my favorite," Kade said.

"And what? She let you lick the pan?"

A smirk lifted Kade's lips. "Nah, she let me kiss the cook."

Lucas snickered.

"What was your excuse?" Derek asked his friend, who still laughed at Kade.

"Nothing I'm willing to discuss in public. Or with you two."

Derek was lucky all three of them were here at all.

While they used to see each other more often, since Kade and Lexie had married and Lucas and Maxie had become engaged, guy time had declined.

Derek got it. Well, he accepted it. He didn't *get* it, as in, he'd never fallen for a woman to the extent he wanted to spend most of his time with her. His thoughts immediately went to Cassie, who he couldn't wait to see on Sunday, before he shook his head hard.

No. Getting a woman out of his system wasn't the same thing as a lifetime commitment.

"Are we ready for some sparring?" Lucas asked.

"Yep."

An hour later, they'd worked up a good sweat and showered in the newly renovated locker rooms.

"Since I've got you two in one place, I wanted to tell you guys something." Derek figured it was as good a time as any to fill them in on what was going on in his life. As Cassie would be around the office now, they deserved to know.

"I agreed to do an in-depth interview." They both knew his reluctance to delve into his past, and he braced himself for the inevitable questions.

Kade paused in tying his sneakers. "What happened to *over my dead body?*" he asked.

"Oh, I know. I saw the gorgeous brunette walking into your office the other day," Lucas said in a knowing tone of voice. "You caved for a piece of ass." He

57

took a towel and snapped it at him.

"It's not like that," Derek shot back. "It's a legitimate opportunity to get the story out my way," he said, uncomfortable because he knew damn well his friend was right. He'd caved for Cassie … who was a hell of a lot more than *a piece of ass*.

"So she was the interviewer?" Lucas pushed, with Kade looking on.

"Just who is this woman?" he asked.

Both men knew Derek's history. They'd been frat brothers, drinking buddies, and knew the whole ugly story of how the rich bitch had treated him. They also knew her name, as well as the fact that Derek had made a play for Storms Consolidated.

He drew a deep breath. "Cassie Storms. From *Take a Byte*," he said, and waited for the backlash.

"You let her sucker you again?" Kade asked.

"Don't be an asshole," Derek muttered. "I'm not the same kid I was. And frankly she's not who I thought she was either."

Kade finished his shoes and rose to his full height. "We're just looking out for you. You hate doing interviews and now you're agreeing, and with someone who may not have your best interest at heart."

"I know what I'm doing. And I expect you two to be friendly when she's in the office."

"I reserve the right to judge her for myself," Kade

insisted.

Lucas glanced at Derek. "You heard the man. Besides, you'd do the same thing for us."

"Did you ever think I can handle myself? I'm getting something out of this too. Information about Storms. The more I know, the better chance I have of talking them into a sale. Through back-door methods, of course."

Kade picked up his bag. "I hope you know what the hell you're doing."

"I do."

"Doesn't hurt that she's a hot piece of ass," Lucas added again. For good measure.

"Don't fucking talk about her that way," Derek warned his friend.

"Yep." Lucas turned to Kade and grinned. "In over his head and we get a front-row seat."

Derek ignore them in part because they were being assholes. And in part because he knew they were right.

SUNDAY ARRIVED WITH snow in the air. It was forecasted to come down later today, but Cassie was still determined to meet Derek to look at apartments. Amanda had offered to join her and offer her opinion on each place, but Cassie had declined.

As much as she needed to find a place to live, the

desire to see Derek again was equally strong, and she wanted time alone with him. She dressed in a cashmere sweater, a pair of tight jeans, and boots and threw on her puffy down jacket. Ready to go, she grabbed her bag and keys, when a knock sounded at her door.

"Coming!" she called, planning to get rid of whichever family member it might be as soon as possible. She had a train to catch.

She opened the door to find Spencer standing on the front porch, wearing a camel coat and a too eager look in his eyes. His dark hair had a dusting of snow, which didn't bode well for her day.

"Hi, sis." He pushed past her and walked inside.

"Whatever happened to calling first?" she muttered, loud enough for him to hear. "I can't talk. I'm on my way out," she said, in case her jacket wasn't enough of a clue.

He shrugged off his own coat and tossed it over a chair near the entry. "That's fine. I wanted to look around and see where I'll be living. What I need to buy and change around."

"It doesn't bother you at all that I was here first? And I have to find a place to go thanks to you?" she asked.

Although she was always aware she was living on her parents' property, she'd decorated the guesthouse just the way she wanted it. She loved so much about the place, from the small study she'd made that overlooked the garden in the summer and the snow banks in the winter to the homey kitchen she'd created for herself to cook in.

"It's my turn, Cass," he said, breaking into her thoughts. "Fair is fair."

Her blood pressure rose at his presumptuousness. "Well, you can come back when I'm home. I don't need you going through my things while I'm out."

"Fine." He picked up his coat. "I'll come by again. Any idea when you'll be moving out?"

She gritted her teeth. "When I find a place to rent and can arrange for movers. Relax and wait your *turn.*" She had to unlock her jaw in order to speak. "Have you gone over any plans for the company? Subscription base is down and—"

"I'll deal with it. It's my job to worry about the company. You can focus on your tech magazine."

She felt his words like a pat on the head, and her anger grew. Apparently her brother was yet another man in her life who had no problem discarding her when she was no longer needed or useful.

Just like Jeremy, who she really hated thinking about. The bastard started working at Storms Consolidated the same year she had, after graduation. He'd been attentive, if on the pushy side, but he'd wined and dined her, and she'd fallen for him. They'd had the same journalistic interest and goals, or so she'd thought. She'd been willing to work her way up the ladder.

His interest in her had waned when she refused to talk to her father about advancing his position within the company. He'd flat out asked her what good she was to him if she wouldn't use her connections to get him a promotion. After all, he'd added, it was for her benefit too. For their future. Yeah. Right.

"Did you get more obnoxious while you were away?" she asked her sibling, heading for the door in order to make her point. They were finished.

"Don't be mad at me. Dad was never going to pick his daughter to run the company. This was a natural, expected change. You should accept it and move on."

If he didn't hold the ultimate say over her job, she might haul off and smack him. Instead she hustled him toward the door and slammed it shut behind him, shaking in the wake of his short visit.

He'd always been a jerk, and his time abroad hadn't made him more of an adult or a decent human being. Nor had her father's handing him the company without him having to earn the position helped. Her father enabled his behavior, and clearly that would never change.

Nostalgia for her grandfather swelled inside her.

God, she missed him. But thinking of him reminded her of the reasons she was sticking around and not finding a regular job with another company. He'd delivered newspapers when he was young and created his own multimedia company as an adult. A self-made man who she admired not just for his business ethics but for the way he treated his family, as well.

Sadly her father had not learned anything from him. But Cassie had. She blew out a long breath and tried to release the stress her brother had brought with him before she headed to the city to find a new place to live.

A little while later, she exited a taxi at the address Derek had given her. The high-rise was located in the upper sixties, a nice neighborhood and not too far from where Storms Consolidated did business. She knew the rent would be high, but her grandfather had set up a trust fund for her that bypassed her father. And though she tried not to rely on anything but her own income, she didn't feel bad dipping into the money to accommodate her forced move.

A security guard sat at the entrance. She gave him her name, and he sent her up to the twenty-first floor, to apartment 2103.

She found the door partially open, knocked once, and entered. "Hello?"

An unfamiliar, well-dressed man with blond hair

walked toward her from inside. "Ms. Storms?"

"Yes."

"I'm Brad Hansen, the property manager." He extended his hand.

"Nice to meet you," she said, shaking his hand.

"Mr. West got hung up with a family emergency. He said he'd meet up with us soon."

"Oh," she said, swallowing over the lump of disappointment, though she did hope everything was okay.

For the next few hours, Brad walked her through three apartments in various buildings, each having different amenities and things to offer. He was good company, knowledgeable about the property and rental details, and they spent an enjoyable afternoon despite the big decision she needed to make.

The snow had picked up, and by the time they made it to the last unit, she knew she was looking at a heavy downfall and it would be smart to head back home soon. They had left the Upper East Side and were now on the West, and she still had to grab a cab or subway back to Penn Station.

She stood in the recently remodeled kitchen. "I have to say this one's my favorite."

"Because of the kitchen? Do you like to cook?" he asked.

"I enjoy it when I have time. I'm sure I'll have

more of it once I live in Manhattan and my commute is cut down," she said, thinking about the positives of this upcoming change.

Because one thing was for certain, she'd have a lot less space. She'd have to store much of her furniture and things, and the thought made her sad. She hadn't realized how lucky she was living in the guesthouse as opposed to a small New York City apartment. She could, if she wanted, buy a house, but she wasn't ready to make that kind of leap.

She turned to Brad. "I need some time to think about which one I want though." Because one on the East Side had more space.

"I totally understand. Nobody expects you to make a decision right away. He gestured toward the door, and she walked to the exit, with him close behind.

He turned to face her. "I realize you need to get home now," he said, pushing open the door. "But would you like to go out some time?" he asked, taking her by surprise.

"Oh. I—"

"Ms. Storms isn't available for the foreseeable future," Derek said from outside the door.

She glanced over to see him standing there, ready to enter as they were walking out. Snow dusted his dark hair and jacket, and he had a scowl on his handsome face.

"Derek!" At this point, she hadn't expected him to show.

"Hansen, I'll take it from here," he said, dismissing the other man.

His cheeks flushed a ruddy color. "Sorry, boss. Didn't realize it was like that." He glanced from Derek to Cassie and back again.

She hadn't realized it either. Nor was she sure how she felt about him staking a claim she hadn't known he'd made. She hadn't planned on saying yes to a date with Brad, but that was something she should be able to decide for herself.

"Brad, thank you for showing me around today. I appreciate it," she said. She'd deal with Derek when they were alone.

"You're welcome. When you make a decision—"

"She'll call *me*," Derek said.

Cassie blinked in surprise. This possessiveness was a new side to Derek, one she hadn't seen before, and it annoyed her as much as it—surprisingly—turned her on.

She waited until Brad had left and headed for the elevator before turning his way. "You didn't need to be rude to him! Besides, I think I can decide for myself whether or not to accept a date."

He raised an eyebrow, looking aggravated and tension-filled, a muscle pulsing in his jaw. "Some things need to be clarified … man to man."

"What are you, a Neanderthal? The man works for you and deserves some respect."

"And now he'll continue to work for me because he knows not to hit on you."

She didn't know whether to be flattered or angry. She settled for annoyed. And a whole lot pleased that he was interested in her enough to stake a claim.

Not that she could let him know that, so she rolled her eyes at his comment. "You didn't have to rush over here. I've seen all the apartments, and Brad was very thorough," she said, complimenting the building manager just to get under Derek's skin.

"Bravo for him. I'll give him a raise," he muttered.

She shook her head. "Okay, caveman," she said, unable to hold back a laugh that broke the tension.

He shoved his hands into his jacket pocket and grinned. "Guess I got a little carried away."

"I'd say so." She met his gaze and turned to a more serious subject. "I hope your family emergency turned out okay?"

His gaze shuttered as he replied, "Fine."

Clearly he had no intention of elaborating, and she wouldn't push him. "I should get going. With the snow, it's going to take me awhile to get back to the train station."

"It's actually pretty bad out. I took my SUV so I

can drive you there. Unless…"

"Unless what?"

"You'd like to forgive my asshole tendencies and have dinner with me."

He treated her to a smile she found incredibly appealing. And sexy. She exhaled a slow puff of air. "I'd like to. Really. But with the weather the way it is, by the time I get back, it'll be hard enough to drive home."

He leaned against the doorframe. "Actually by the time the train gets you back, it'll be dangerous for you to drive on the roads. The weather on Long Island is blizzard conditions."

"Oh, no." She ran a hand through her ponytail and groaned. "I should have paid more attention."

"The storm shifted during the day. I'm not sure you could have planned for this."

"So what are my choices? Have dinner with you and stay over in a hotel?" She bit down on her lower lip, knowing she hadn't planned for the possibility. No change of clothes, no toiletries.

"That's one possibility. Or I have a guest room. You're more than welcome to stay over. My sister leaves things for when she sleeps in the city, so I'm sure you'll be comfortable. I'll even be on my best behavior." His light blue eyes gleamed with a promise she didn't want him to keep.

"Hmm." She obviously needed to remain in town, so the only question was where. "Decisions, decisions. A hotel room all to myself for the night with room service and movies. Or hang out with you."

"Come on, princess. Live a little."

"Princess?"

He shrugged. "It's what I used to call you—in my mind—way back when." His cheeks turned red and she flushed in response.

Princess, huh? Well, she supposed there were worse things he could call her. "I think I'll take the hotel."

"Seriously?"

No, she thought, but it really was fun to push his buttons. "You said to live a little. I just thought you meant to treat myself to the finer things."

"I'll treat you to the finer things," he muttered. "You're staying with me."

"Yes sir, caveman." She grinned, pleased with their easy banter.

And the fact that she was staying over at his place. She had a chance to get to know him better. To lay out the parameters for the interview. And who knew what else might happen between them.

She certainly knew what her fantasies demanded. Ever since he'd come back into her life, her dreams had been more vivid.

And arousing.

Dream Derek had magic hands that slid over her body in a sensual caress. With his mouth, he sucked her nipples and pinched with his fingers, until waves of desire pounded at her, her body seconds from an intense climax. And when he thrust inside her, she came immediately, her skin, her entire being consumed with passion.

She'd wake up, tangled in sheets, a light coating of sweat on her body, her breasts heavy, her sex tingling in the most delightful of ways.

She trembled at the memories, suddenly aware she stood in an apartment hallway, Derek staring at her intently. "You're flushed. Do I *want* to know what you're thinking?"

Definitely not, she thought. "Let's go see what the weather's like," she said, not meeting his gaze.

"Your wish is my command," he said, an amused smile on his handsome face as he turned to lock up the apartment and follow her to the elevator.

# Chapter Four

B Y THE TIME they exited the building, the snow
was coming down in heavy drifts. The weather-
men had definitely underestimated this storm, Derek
thought, grateful for their mistake that gave him Cassie
all to himself.

He nearly hadn't made it at all. His mother hadn't
been feeling well, and his sister had taken her to the
hospital. It turned out to be indigestion, thank God,
but he'd spent the better part of the day in the emergency room. Not something he wanted to get into
with Cassie.

When he thought about his mother being a widow,
his father long gone, the anger he felt for her family
resurfaced. Given their history, the only way to be
with her was to keep the past where it belonged, to
remember that whatever happened between them
could only be short term. But for now, she seemed as

eager to spend the night with him as he was to be with her.

Thank God, after the way he'd behaved earlier. Almost thirty years old and he'd never acted like a possessive idiot over a woman. Apparently he wasn't too old to start that shit now. Brad had been standing too close, and he'd been too interested in Cassie, beyond wanting to rent her the apartment. Something inside Derek had snapped, causing him to stake his claim, like the caveman she'd accused him of being.

They were quiet on the trip to his apartment because he needed all his concentration on the road. Which didn't mean he wasn't fully aware of the woman in the passenger seat, looking adorable in a pink fluffy down jacket, melted snowflakes making her hair damp, and the cold having turned her nose red before they reached his home. Her vanilla perfume took over the car, enveloping him in her arousing scent and causing his cock to become erect and uncomfortable when he needed to focus.

Finally, after a skid and inching his way, he made it to the parking garage beneath his building. He left his car with Manny, the attendant, and led Cassie to the elevator that took them to his seventeenth-floor apartment.

After growing up poor, he hadn't skimped on luxury or amenities when choosing where he wanted to live and how he wanted to furnish.

Before he inserted the key in the door, he turned toward her. "I should warn you—"

Before he could say another word, loud barking sounds came from inside the apartment.

"A dog!" she exclaimed, clapping her hands together. "I love them."

"Brace yourself," he muttered, pushing open the door.

Derek's thirty-five-pound wheaten terrier greeted them, hopping on his back paws, his front ones leaning on Cassie's thighs as he jumped up and down, begging for attention.

"Meet Oscar," he said, knowing better than to bother with a stern *down*. "Oscar, be nice," he said, aware the two-year-old dog wouldn't be deterred from his wheaten greeting nor would he calm down until he'd said his hellos.

"Oh my God, he's so cute," Cassie said, trying to pet Oscar while he did his happy-to-see-you dance.

"Do you need to take him for a walk?" Cassie asked.

He glanced at his watch. "The dog walker probably just took him, considering he's damp. I'm sure she left a note. Take off your coat and make yourself at home," Derek said.

He headed over to the credenza and dropped his

keys, scanning the note the dog walker had, in fact, left. Unfortunately it contained more than information about walking, eating, and Oscar's business. His dog walker, who had been amazing and reliable for over two years, had given him notice. She was moving out of state with her fiancé.

"Shit."

"What's wrong?" Cassie asked, jacket in hand.

He opened the closet and hung up their outerwear. He slipped off his shoes and she did the same.

"My dog walker gave notice. She's moving. I have no idea how I'm going to find someone good, and willing to deal with Oscar's … exuberant personality," he said, giving his dog a pat.

Oscar who, on hearing his name, had raised himself up on his hind legs once more.

Cassie followed him into his apartment, Oscar on her heels. "There's an app called Rover. It's like Uber for dog walkers. You can find someone who is vetted and rated that way. I have friends who've used the service."

"Oh, I've heard of them. As an app guy, I have to say I'm impressed. I'll look into it. Thanks."

"Happy to help."

"So, do you like pizza? Downstairs on the corner is the best pizza ever. And they deliver."

"Love it. Pepperoni if you don't mind."

"Exactly what I'd order." He pulled out his cell phone and called a number he had on speed dial and placed the order.

He showed her the guest room, hoping she wouldn't be using that bed, rather sleeping in his—without a lot of REM sleep being achieved—and they settled in his big family room/den in front of his big-screen TV, behind which was a wall of windows.

Snow came down in big chunks, creating a gorgeous vista in the background, but he couldn't tear his gaze from Cassie. She curled her legs beneath her and settled into the corner of the couch, Oscar snuggled by her side.

Traitor.

Not that Derek blamed him. He wanted to be close enough to breathe in her warm scent and feel her body heat against his skin. His cock wasn't happy being adjusted and forced to ignore the desire he felt just looking at the swell of her breasts in the formfitting sweater, but he managed to deal.

They made small talk about the apartments while waiting for dinner, discussed his business while eating pizza and drinking a beer—for old time's sake. Even he couldn't help but laugh at the reminder of her first taste out of the bottle.

After cleaning up and him taking Oscar for a quick walk, they resettled in to watch a movie. Oscar crashed on his doggie bed, giving Derek his first opening to sit close to Cassie.

He had every intention of making his move, when she cleared her throat and asked, "So I know you don't want to talk about the family emergency you had earlier today, but I've been meaning to ask, how are your parents? It's been so long since I've seen them."

He froze, his hand halfway to the television remote. "My parents?"

"Yes. I haven't seen them since I left for school. I know they left because they got another job but—"

Derek sat upright, all thoughts of touching her, kissing her, gone. "That subject is off-limits."

She flinched and inched back against the seat. "I don't understand."

His first instinct was to revert to how he'd thought about her for years. A cruel girl only too happy to humiliate him, but he forced himself to draw a calming breath. And to remember that the Cassie he knew appeared to be kind and caring.

"My father ... died years ago. I don't like to talk about it."

"Oh, Derek, I'm sorry. I know how close you were." She linked her hands behind her head and leaned back, meeting his gaze, sadness and understanding in her eyes.

Shit. Now he felt bad for snapping at her. And

when he looked into her warm brown eyes, another emotion took hold. Desire flooded his veins, all thoughts of anything but getting her into his arms gone.

She stared into his eyes, and his will to fight the attraction evaporated, and before he knew it, his mouth was on hers.

CASSIE'S HEAD WAS spinning. From his whiplash change in attitude to the news he'd given about his father to the kiss he placed on her lips, her emotions had been pulled in different directions. But with that one touch, she softened and fell into his kiss. She loved how he possessed her, with a combined forcefulness that turned her on and a gentleness that melted her panties.

He pulled at the elastic around her hair, releasing the ponytail so her hair fell over her shoulders. He brushed through the long strands with his fingertips, tugging at her scalp with each successive brush.

His tongue slid between her lips and tangled with hers, as he continued to seduce her with long, luxurious kisses that had her head spinning and her body going along for the ride. He grasped her hair in one hand, tilting her head to one side and trailing seductive sweeps of his tongue along her jawline, her throat, working his way down to her collarbone.

She trembled, her nipples tightening into hardened peaks, arousal gliding through her body in luxurious waves of desire. He nipped at her collarbone and licked his way back up her neck and throat, nuzzling at her ear. And all the while, all she could do was let him have his way, her body liquid in his arms.

Since Jeremy, she'd been selective to the point of not making it past one date before breaking up with a man, so it had been a long time since she'd been with a guy like this. In fact, she'd go so far as to say no man had made her feel so hot so quickly.

She slid her hands to his sides, pushing up his sweater and bracing her palms on his heated skin. She brushed her thumbs upward, and he groaned, his mouth coming down hard on hers once more. His kisses were hard, more feverish, and he pressed her back against the cool leather couch, his body coming down on hers. His masculine scent permeated her senses.

His erection aligned with her sex while his mouth did wicked things to hers. He lifted her shirt, pulling it up and over her head but trapping her arms in the soft wool.

Through the lace, he brushed his thumbs over her distended nipples, causing them to pucker harder, and she felt the answering contractions deep inside her body.

"So pretty," he murmured, leaning down and pulling a lace-covered bud into his mouth and tugging with his teeth.

She groaned and jerked her hands, but they were twisted in the sweater and she was at his mercy, unable to touch in return.

"You don't play fair."

"As long as I'm playing, I'm happy," he said, taking a nip of the other nipple before laving it with his tongue.

Her body quivered with need and she yanked harder, freeing her hands and tossing the garment to the floor. She ran her hands over his broad shoulders, his sweater preventing her from feeling his skin.

As if reading her mind, he pulled it off, baring his chest. The stuff of fantasies, she thought, gliding her hands over his hair-roughened flesh, allowing her nails to rake over his nipples.

He groaned and kissed her once more before sitting up, bracing his knees on either side of her body. Raising himself up enough to give him leverage, he flicked open the button on her jeans, sliding down the zipper. He eased his hand into her bikini underwear. She moaned at the touch of his fingers against her sex.

He raised his hips. "Lift," he instructed.

She complied, allowing him to pull her jeans down

until they were stuck on her hips. He didn't seem to care, his gaze intent on her damp panties. "You're wet," he murmured. "All for me."

Her cheeks burned at his frank talk.

"Let's see the rest." He pulled her panties down, exposing her sex.

"Bare. So sweet." He slid his fingers over her outer lips, and she arched her back and moaned out loud.

He grasped her thighs and pulled her legs as wide as her restrictive clothing would let them go. She was a combination of embarrassed and beyond turned on.

"You're beautiful when you blush," he said, jarring her because she hadn't realized he was watching her face.

"You're just so … frank."

"And honest. I like looking at you. Any reason I shouldn't tell you?" he asked as he began to play with her sex, sliding the moisture all around until she was coated with her own juices.

He didn't wait for an answer. Instead he pressed his thumb against her clit, and stars flashed behind her eyes. She lost all inhibition and embarrassment because he focused on the one place sure to send her flying. He slid a long finger inside her, and her body contracted around him. His finger felt good but it wasn't enough. She needed more thickness, more friction in order to come.

And she needed to climax badly. He pumped a finger in and out of her core, his thumb circling over her clit again, alternatively pressing down, moving in maddening circles, pausing so he could fuck her with his finger. Her entire body shook as her climax neared.

He'd found his rhythm, and between the digit inside her and the hard press and grind on her sex, she was lost in sensation. Her entire being, her focus came down to that one sensitive spot.

He pumped harder. Pressed more insistently. And when he curled his finger against her inner wall, finding that elusive spot, she came hard.

"Derek, Derek! God!" White stars exploded behind her eyes, her entire body shook, and she cried out, his name a chant on her lips.

Suddenly the dog started barking, startling her. Derek jumped at the sound, levering himself up and off her. "Jesus, Oscar, quiet!"

The dog barked some more, so he headed over and calmed Oscar, murmuring to the canine until he whined and settled back into his bed.

On his way back, he bent down, picked up her sweater, and handed her the garment, a grin on his handsome face.

"What?" she asked.

"You came so hard you scared the dog."

Once again tonight, her face flushed with embarrassment. "How kind of you to point that out."

"Sorry. Here. Let me help you up."

She accepted the gesture and allowed him to pull her to a sitting position. Cassie slid her panties and jeans back on, followed by drawing her sweater over her head.

He rejoined her on the couch. "I guess Oscar isn't used to … entertainment." He chuckled and held up one hand. "I'm not laughing *at* you. I'm being serious. I don't usually bring women here. He's not used to—"

"Why don't we let it go," she suggested, her lips lifting in a smile despite it all.

Derek settled back on the sofa, sliding one arm behind her shoulders, pulling her against him. "Okay, but I appreciate you being such a good sport."

She grinned. "It's not his fault. Besides … I think I owe him a thank you." She wasn't sure how much further things would have gone between them if Oscar hadn't interrupted, and the fact was… "I don't mean to be a tease, but I'm not ready for … more."

Not that she didn't want to sleep with him. She did. Oh, how she did. As hard as he'd made her come, she'd felt empty without him inside her, filling her while the waves crashed over her body. But her mind and her heart were a little slower to catch up. For one thing, Derek ran hot and cold with her, and that made her wary.

He brushed her hair off her shoulders and pressed a kiss against her cheek. "I wouldn't pressure you tonight."

She tilted her head, meeting his gaze. "If we're being honest, it's been awhile for me. I got hurt pretty badly and I've been careful ever since. I don't just—"

"Sleep with any guy you meet." He curled her hair around his fingers and brushed his thumb over the strands. "I think I figured that out about you from the get-go."

She grasped his hand, trying to show him she appreciated his understanding. "I'm glad you get it. Some guys don't."

"I'm not some guy. Besides, I said I wouldn't pressure you tonight. Not that there wouldn't be a next time."

Pleasure and a warm sense of gratitude washed over her. "I'm very glad to hear that," she said, wanting him to understand that no for now didn't necessarily mean no for good. "Because I never said I couldn't be persuaded."

DEREK DIDN'T SLEEP well. In part because he had a raging hard-on that not even his hand helped abate, but also because the woman he desired slept a wall away. Early the next morning, he pulled on a pair of

jeans and a sweatshirt, planning to head out and take
Oscar for his morning walk. But as he brushed his
teeth and got ready, he couldn't stop going over the
events of last night.

Cassie had been a revelation. There was an innate
sweetness about her he'd never experienced before.
Despite how he'd all but snarled at her when she'd
asked about his parents, she had been genuinely sorry
for him and caring about his loss. Which made her a
nicer person than he was, that was for damned sure.

And watching her come apart in his arms affected
him more than any experience he'd had before. And
that threw him, making the fact that Oscar had interrupted what would have come after, namely him
stripping off his clothes and burying himself deep
inside her wet heat, a good thing. Something they both
would have regretted come morning.

Another reason she stood out to him. She wasn't
eager to jump into his bed. To sleep with a billionaire.
To use him for his money. And he sensed her lack of
greed had little to do with her having money of her
own. She was just that genuine a person.

Which didn't make his waffling feelings toward her
easy to deal with. Nor did it help his conscience.
Especially since she'd admitted to being betrayed in
the past. He didn't want to hurt her too, but he still
wanted to acquire her father's company and run it into

the ground. He just felt more guilt about it now.

With his mind heavy, he quietly made his way to the family room, where Oscar slept if he chose not to join Derek in his bed. The dog bed was empty. Which meant there was only one place the traitor could be.

In the room where Cassie slept.

He ran a hand through his hair, debating whether to knock or open the door and let the dog slide through. It sounded quiet, so he turned the knob and glanced in. Sunlight began to stream through the slats in the window shades, casting a golden glow on Cassie's brown hair. She slept on.

As for Oscar, instead of bounding toward him as Derek expected, the dog lay tangled around Cassie's feet.

"Come on," Derek whispered roughly.

Oscar raised his head and whined. Hell. If Derek were wrapped around Cassie, he wouldn't want to leave either. But the dog needed his morning walk or he'd pee on the floor when he finally got his lazy ass out of bed.

Derek shook the leash in his hand. No luck.

He padded into the room, wearing only socks on his feet, trying to remain quiet. "Oscar, come," he tried again, using his stern indoor voice.

"Derek?" Cassie murmured, pulling herself up against the pillows, taking the comforter with her.

One glance told him why. Her shoulders were bare beneath the covers, and when he guessed what was underneath, his mouth went dry. If he'd thought about the fact that she was naked next door, he wouldn't have made it through the night.

"Sorry. Need to walk the dog." He leaned over and hooked the leash onto Oscar's collar, at which point Oscar rolled over onto his back, making himself dead weight.

Stupid shit. Derek couldn't help but laugh.

"He likes me," she said on a giggle.

He wasn't the only one, Derek thought. A few more tugs and Oscar grumbled his way off the bed. "I'll be back in a little while. I'll bring up muffins too."

She treated him to a grateful smile. "Thank you. And thanks for the toothbrush and everything in the bathroom last night."

He nodded. "Maybe next time you'll find all the necessities in my room," he said, then pulled on the leash and headed out of the room before she could reply.

# Chapter Five

C ASSIE WAITED UNTIL Derek left the room before falling back against the pillows and closing her eyes. Staying alone here had been difficult last night, especially after she'd peeled off her clothing and climbed into bed naked. Well, with her panties on, but no way was she sleeping in a bra. Ouch. But knowing Derek was next door and she was in here with barely a stitch of clothes made it difficult to stick to her resolve to get to know him better before sleeping with him.

She'd persevered … until he'd shown up in her room this morning, unshaven, wearing jeans and a sweatshirt, looking sexy as hell while he tried to wrangle his dog for a walk. He wasn't the billionaire the world wanted to know better, he was a damned fine-looking man she wanted to know intimately.

She blew out a harsh breath, climbed out of bed, and got ready for the day. By the time she walked into the kitchen, Derek had returned. They ate muffins and coffee, a blessing to her rumbling stomach.

"Did the weather clear up?" she asked.

He nodded. "The sun is shining and the roads are clear. Can I give you a ride back home?"

She had no intention of being stubborn and sitting on a train. "Thank you. I'd appreciate it."

"Mind if Oscar hops in the back? He loves the car and doesn't get to drive around much because we live in the city." He gestured to the dog who lay frog-legged on the floor, staring up at her with moony eyes.

She did her best not to laugh. "I'd love the company." She knelt down and petted the dog's furry back, and he rolled over for a belly rub.

A smile lifted the corners of Derek's mouth. "You have a fan."

"He kept me warm last night," she said. And she'd enjoyed the sensation of the big, comfortable body against her legs.

"I would have kept you warm." Derek glanced at her, his gaze simmering at his more sensual meaning.

"Maybe I wish I'd let you," she admitted, her nipples tightening beneath the soft sweater. She'd held off for reasons that still made sense, but a part of her knew she wanted more from Derek than a one-night stand. She liked him a lot. And she wanted to see where things could go.

A pleased smile lit his handsome face, giving her hope he felt the same way.

"There'll be another time," he assured her with a wink, and her stomach flipped in the most pleasant way while her sex had a clenching reaction of its own.

A little while later, with Oscar in the back, hooked up to his seat belt harness, panting in her ear, they headed for Long Island.

"You know, there's a park near the house where you can take Oscar off-leash. He'd love the snow. And I'd love to see him flying around with the white stuff all over him."

He laughed. "Sounds like a date."

She liked the sound of that idea. He pulled off the familiar highway exit to her house. "So … is it okay if I shadow you at your office this week?" she asked, bringing up the interview. "I'd like to see what a normal day in the life is like. Plus, I can talk to your assistant and partners, if that's okay with you."

He grumbled something under his breath.

"Now you sound like Oscar when you asked him to do something he didn't want to do."

He shot her a sideways look before turning back to the road. "Yes, you can shadow me."

"Thank you." She already knew he wouldn't enjoy the process, but it was necessary.

From memory, he drove the back roads to the estate, but when they reached the secondary driveway that led to her house, it hadn't yet been plowed. "Can you pull through the gate and drop me off at the front of the main house? I'll go through the back. I hope they at least shoveled the walking path."

"Hard to get good help these days, hmm?" he asked sarcastically. His father used to shovel the walkways and plow the driveways.

She ignored the comment.

He pulled into the driveway and put the car in park.

She bit down on her lower lip. "You know, if we're going to spend time together apart from the interview, you're going to have to really get past our history, and at this point, I'm not sure you have."

She reached for the handle before turning around to face him once more, her heart pounding hard in her chest. "I'm not giving up on the interview. But you should think about whether or not you want to see me outside of a working relationship. Because I don't want to deal with the snide remarks and sudden change of temperature when something you don't like comes up."

She yanked open the door as he called her name.

"Cassie, wait."

She ignored him, climbing out of the car and slamming the door shut behind her. Within the last twenty-four hours, he'd snapped at her twice, and she didn't appreciate it. Let him deal with *her* attitude for a change.

He met her around her side of the car, grasping her by the shoulders. "I'm sorry."

"Maybe you are. For the moment. I just don't know if you can really separate us now from the past. You need to think about it. And I need to get inside. It's cold," she said, grabbing on to the excuse she needed.

Although it was warmer than yesterday, her nose was already cold from the wind. And Derek did need time to think.

He released her and she headed for the front door. "Thank you for last night," she said over her shoulder.

"Cassie—"

Instead of answering, she lifted a hand in a wave before letting herself into the house, aware of her snow-covered boots on the marble floor. She shut the door behind her and blew out a long breath.

She released the zipper on her jacket as a combination of sadness and anticipation rolled through her. Who knew what decisions Derek would make about her once he gave it some thought. Still, she didn't regret her outburst. She didn't want a man who was only half in when it came to anything beyond business between them. She'd had enough of relationships built on lies and partial truths about the other person's motives.

"Where have you been?" Spencer asked, walking out of the study to the left of the front door.

"You scared me!"

"I was doing work when I saw the car pull up by the front door. Who was that guy? New boyfriend?"

"None of your business! What's wrong with you? I don't question your relationships."

He raised one eyebrow over eyes the same brown as her own. "Oh, so it's a relationship."

"I didn't say that."

He studied her, his gaze going from her feet, all the way up. "You didn't have to. You're in the same clothes you were in when I came by your house yesterday."

She bit down on the inside of her cheek. "I got snowed in while I was in the city looking at apartments so you can move in."

"So who drove you home? Your broker? Come on, sis, fess up."

"Fine, it was Derek West," she said, if only to shut her brother up. "I'm interviewing him for *Take a Byte*, and he was kind enough to help me find a place to live."

"Are you fucking kidding me? The gardener's kid?"

She stiffened at the disdain in Spencer's tone.

"No, the *self-made* billionaire," she countered, hoping her brother got the hint that his own wealth hadn't been earned.

God, what was wrong with men? She'd had enough of the class difference bullshit with Derek, though his had been more subtle and more personal.

"You can do better than him."

"And you don't care who I see, so why do you have a problem with him?"

As if he was suddenly uncomfortable, Spencer rolled his shoulders and unbuttoned the top button on his shirt. "It's just awkward. They used to work for us until Dad caught his mother stealing. You need to stay away from them."

"Whoa. Wait. What?"

"His mother's a thief. Of course, she got away with it, but Dad let them go, no references. Which is what they deserved. So steer clear."

Nausea filled her throat. "No. I don't believe that." His mother was the sweetest, kindest woman. She wouldn't steal from them. "Dad told me they moved on to a new job."

He shifted from foot to foot. "I guess they didn't want to upset you. You always were too nice to the help."

That was it. She wanted to go home, to her house, while it was still hers. "You're a pig. Please tell me the walkway is shoveled so I can get home."

"Yes. The snowplow broke. They're coming back later to do the secondary driveway."

"Good. I'm going home."

"Find an apartment?" he asked.

"When I move out, you'll be the first to know." She turned and walked away, consumed by the information he'd provided.

She didn't know the whole story and probably never would. Not from her family, but she now understood why Derek resented her so much. And if she'd held out any hope, subconsciously or otherwise, that he'd come around and want a relationship, her brother had shattered those dreams.

Derek might give her an interview. He might even want to sleep with her. But he'd never find her good enough for anything more.

DEREK HAD FUCKED up. How else could he explain why, when he had Cassie right where he wanted her, after an intimate night, on a morning where she was considering taking things to the next level, he'd opened his big mouth and put up a barrier between them? He couldn't keep letting the past get in the way, and there was only one person he could talk to about his issues.

Although he didn't want to upset his mom, he reminded himself she'd had indigestion, not a heart attack. And she'd always been there for him. Always.

He drove out to the small house on the south shore of Long Island that he'd bought her with his first real earnings from Blink. His dad had already been gone, and she'd refused anything huge and elaborate. Derek's sister had married and lived close by, which gave him a sense of relief that she was never truly alone should she need anything.

As usual, he found his mom in the state-of-the-art kitchen. The split-level house might be small, but Derek made sure his mom lacked for nothing in the details.

"I'm so glad you're here!" His mom pulled off her apron and met him with a big hug.

He squeezed her hard, then stepped back to study her. "I suppose it would be too much to ask for you to rest after the scare you had?"

She looked up at him, her blue eyes so like his own. "Rest after indigestion? I'm embarrassed and want to forget the whole thing."

"Better safe than sorry," he assured her.

"Come, sit. Can I make you a cup of coffee?"

"Sure," he said, because he was chilled and because his mother was happiest when she was doing for her children. "And what kind of cake do you have?" His mother always had fresh-baked goods on hand.

"Coffee cake," she said with a laugh.

"Big slice, please."

She smiled, thrilled with his answer. "So," she said as she puttered around the kitchen, brewing them both a cup of hot coffee, "to what do I owe this visit? Checking up on your old mother?"

He took in her still-jet-black hair, pulled back in a bun, and her barely lined face. She wore a pair of jeans and an old sweatshirt, with fuzzy slippers on her feet. Old? Not a chance, not in looks or demeanor.

"No, actually. I wanted to talk to you." She placed his cup on the counter and he wrapped his hands around the extra-large mug. "Someone came back into my life recently and it has me … mixed up," he admitted.

After slicing two pieces of cake, Derek's big enough for two, she pulled her chair close to his and sat down. "Who is this person who has my normally unflappable son ruffled?" she asked.

He drew a deep breath. "Cassie Storms."

"Oh. Oh!"

She descended into silence, and he let her mull over the information, which undoubtedly brought back a host of bad memories.

"She was always such a sweet child," his mother said, her first reaction taking him off guard.

He'd never shared what happened that day with anyone but Kade and Lucas. Back then he'd been too embarrassed by the comments, which, though humiliating, had also been true. No rich girl was going to bring the gardener's son home to Daddy.

He took a long sip of hot coffee, letting it warm him from the inside out. "Do you hold a grudge?" he asked his mom.

"Against Cassandra?"

He smiled at the use of her full name. "Against any of the family. But yes, Cassie too."

"God, no. Cassie was away at school when *it* happened. She was nothing but a respectful, nice girl, so no. I don't hold a grudge against her." His mother studied him with a curious look in her eyes. "As for the others, Daniella Storms was blinded by her husband. She always was. Like Cassandra, though, she treated me with respect. And she wasn't home the day Christopher Storms called the police and accused me of stealing."

"What?"

She shook her head. "She was away for a spa week with some of her women friends. I never heard from her, but she had nothing to do with what happened either."

"Hmm." Derek processed that information, filing it away because he couldn't help but sense it was important. How, he didn't know. Yet.

She rubbed her hands together. "You know, life's too short to hold grudges, but if you're asking me if I like or respect Mr. Storms, the answer is a definite no. After years of service and no issues, the man railroaded me without a second thought. And it wasn't good enough to fire me. He called the police too. He and his son stood by, watching me taken away." She shook her head, her eyes downcast at the memory.

He placed a hand over hers. "I'm sorry to bring all this up again."

She brushed off his statement with a wave of her hand. "How did you come to see Cassandra again?" she asked.

"She called the office. Turns out she wanted to interview me."

His mother nodded. "I see. And did you do the interview?"

"We're just beginning. She's looking for something more in-depth than a one-time conversation."

"So you're spending time with her and the past is getting in the way?" his mother astutely asked.

"That's part of it." He dug into the cake, needing a big bite of fortification for the rest of this conversation.

"And the other part?" His mother pushed for information.

Derek swallowed the delicious piece of cake and followed it up with another sip of coffee. "We're spending time together aside from work, and that's why the past is coming between us."

"Oh, good lord," his mother murmured. "Christopher Storms would have a coronary if he knew."

"Is that wishful thinking?" Derek asked wryly.

His mother shot him a warning look. Yeah, yeah. He knew. Don't wish anyone ill.

But he hadn't considered what Cassie's family would think about them seeing each other, mostly because he hadn't initially considered them getting together anything more than a fling. Getting her out of his system so he'd stop obsessing about the gorgeous girl with the big brown eyes. That long, luxurious hair. The breasts he couldn't keep his hands off and the body he craved entry to.

Shit. These were not the thoughts to have around his mother. But they certainly proved his biggest issue. He wasn't getting Cassie *out of his system* any time soon.

"Oh, son, you have it bad, don't you?" his mother asked, a knowing smile on her face.

"What? No. It's just—"

"Don't lie to your mother," she said, the words a verbal slap. She always did know when he wasn't telling the truth. "You can't hold Cassie responsible for what her father did."

"No, that's not her fault, any more than the fact that I was the maid and the gardener's son," he said, admitting more of what was bothering him.

His mother pursed her lips. "Facts are what facts are. Either you can live with them or you can't."

"That's pretty much what Cassie said."

She nodded. "Smart girl. You need to move on from the past. Holding a grudge isn't going to bring your father back," she said, hitting on the crux of all he hadn't said.

An immediate lump formed in his throat, his chest heavy with sadness. His father had developed a hacking cough that he treated with over-the-counter cough medicine. He continued to work at menial jobs, the only ones he could get without references for his past years of work. By the time he started coughing blood and did seek treatment, he was diagnosed him with incurable lung cancer. Too much time had passed with him undiagnosed and untreated.

"Don't you ever wonder, if things had been different, if you'd both had jobs and health insurance, if he would still be alive today?"

She blinked in surprise. "What? No. Derek, your father was a stubborn man. There's no saying he would have gone to the doctor any sooner."

He reared back in shock. All these years he'd believed one narrative. "I always thought if he'd just had insurance, things would have been different."

"Because it was easier to blame someone else."

"I still blame Christopher Storms."

"If that helps you sleep at night, go ahead. But don't add Cassandra to the list."

He pushed the cake plate away, his appetite gone. "Thanks for the talk," he said, appreciating his mother's honesty.

"You're welcome. But I want to add one more thing, and you might not like what I have to say." She tipped her head to the side and eyed him like only a parent could.

"Go on."

"Just because the past shouldn't be barrier to whatever's going on between you and Cassie doesn't mean it won't be. Her father is a first-class bastard. No matter how much money you have now, he'll never see you as good enough for his girl."

The sad truth was, her own father wasn't good enough to his only daughter. But that fact only bolstered his mother's point. The man was an ass. And Derek still wasn't good enough to bring home to Daddy.

The only question remained, would Cassie still care?

He shook his head, realizing he was getting way ahead of himself. He hadn't even slept with her yet.

Why was he contemplating such serious shit?

Because she wasn't the kind of woman you toyed with. He'd known that at eighteen, and he understood it even more now.

DEREK LOOKED OVER the building tops through his office window. The sun shone on the snow-covered landscape, while behind him, Oscar slept beneath his desk. Derek placed his hand on the cold window and acknowledged to himself his conversation with his mother was never far from his mind. He'd been mulling it over ever since, and he always came to the same conclusion.

He wanted Cassie. He couldn't see past the here and now … and he didn't need to. If they clicked, he'd deal with what came next. If they didn't, she'd be purged from his system.

It was time to get his act together and bring his A game. Like he had the night of their first date. But first he needed to apologize.

Good thing she was coming to his office this morning, and he knew just the way to prove to her he'd heard her words and taken them to heart.

He picked up the phone on his desk. "Becky, ask Kade and Lucas to get their asses in here please."

"You got it."

He loved the informal atmosphere here and the fact that his assistant put up with him.

Two minutes later, he had his partners in the room. Their presence woke Oscar, and he greeted them with what breed lovers called the Wheaten Greetin'. He flew across the room, hopping on his hind legs, bouncing and licking at each of the men.

"Get down, mutt," Lucas said, affection in his voice as he stood, braced for impact.

Kade rubbed Oscar's head. "Why do we have the dog for company today?"

Derek put his hand against the back of his neck. "That's part of why I wanted to talk to you. Cassie's coming by this morning, and I need you two to answer any questions she has."

Kade folded his arms across his chest. "As long as she answers any questions I have first. I need to make sure she's not taking advantage of my friend."

Derek rolled his eyes. "I'm asking you to behave. For my sake. I'm the one who screwed up. Letting you two talk to her is one way I'm apologizing."

Lucas grinned. "Fine. We'll tell her what an asshole you were back in college. A code-loving nerd."

"Works for me," Derek muttered, knowing he wouldn't get anything better from these two jerks now, but they'd behave later with Cassie. Which was all that mattered.

"On another subject, I'm getting married," Lucas announced.

"We know. You put a ring on it a few months ago," Derek said.

"No, I'm getting married soon. Like, on Valentine's Day. Maxie and I don't want to wait until the baby is born. We want it all legal ahead of time. Plus, I can't wait to make that woman my wife. So will you two be my best man? Men? Would you stand up there with me?" he asked, chuckling.

"You know we will," Derek said, pulling his friend into a brotherly hug before Kade did the same.

"We're keeping it small. You know, because Maxie isn't close with her parents."

Derek understood. Their situation was complicated. It was a miracle they were getting married at all, Derek thought. Lucas and Maxie had had their timing all wrong, Maxie having been married to Lucas's asshole brother, who'd all but tricked her into being with him. They should have been together all along. But now not only were they a couple, they were having a baby. They were a real family, as it should have always been.

"I'm happy for you," Derek said.

"I'm happy for me," Lucas admitted.

"What about you? How's the missus?" he asked Kade.

"Fucking great. I highly recommend marriage," he said with a stupid grin.

Derek shook his head. "And Lexie's sister? Is Kendall holding steady?" Kendall was bipolar and was on an upswing after an extended stay at an inpatient facility for treatment.

"Thank God, she's fantastic too. She's walking dogs for people in our building and working at a shelter. Holding down a job, taking her meds," he said with pride.

"And staying away from Julian?" Lucas asked.

"Yes. She was hurt enough by that bastard," Kade muttered, his fingers flexing at just the mention of the man's name.

Julian, one of their college friends who'd been in on the inception of Blink but who'd succumbed to a drug addiction instead of focusing on the billion-dollar prize. He'd reared his head when Blink was ready to go public, almost ruined Kade, and used Kendall, Lexie's sister, to do it. Most recently, he'd tried to contact Kendall again, something all three men swore they wouldn't let happen.

"Speaking of dogs, you still haven't explained why Oscar's here. Not that I don't like him, but you don't normally bring him to the office," Lucas said.

"He's here because Cassie likes him," Derek admitted.

"And you need to butter her up. Got it," Lucas said, laughing.

Derek turned to Kade, who remained silent on the subject of Cassie. "Did you say Kendall is walking dogs? Because if so, I need her phone number. Oscar's walker quit."

"She'd love to do it. I'll shoot you her info on your cell later."

"Thank you. And now, if you don't mind…"

"You want to be alone when Cassie gets here. Got it," Lucas said. "We'd laugh at you except we can't. We've been where you are."

"What? No. I'm not that—"

"Involved?" Kade asked, glancing down at the dog who had never been to the office before.

"Out!" Derek pointed to the door, and his friends left, laughing.

A few minutes later, Becky announced Cassie's arrival. Derek rose as the door opened, and she walked in, looking every inch the professional interviewer. From the way her hair was pulled up to the dark pencil skirt and heels and through to the white blouse, she was prim and proper—except for the hint of cleavage revealed by the open buttons. An enticing hint that had him licking his lips, the memory of her taste strong.

"Good morning," he said, walking around and

meeting her by the door.

"Good morning." She smiled warily. He didn't blame her. Their last parting hadn't been a great one.

No sooner had she spoken than Oscar heard her voice, jumped up, and greeted her with his bounding enthusiasm before flopping to the floor.

"Hey, pal!" She knelt by his side to give him a belly rub.

While she gave the dog attention, Derek shut the office door and locked them inside.

"What's Oscar doing here?" she asked, rising to her feet.

He opted for the truth. "I thought he'd help me break the ice."

"Look, I know what I said to you the other day, but the truth is, it's not for me to dictate how you behave or what you say. It is for me to decide what I want to put up with. And—"

"I'm sorry," he said before she could tell him she didn't want to see him outside of this extended interview.

She blinked, long lashes fluttering over her big brown eyes. "You are?"

"You're not the only one who can admit when they were wrong." He managed a smile. It wasn't easy to swallow his pride. He wasn't a man used to humbling himself for someone else.

But she'd taught him the value of apologizing. Of what it meant to the person on the receiving end. He grasped her shoulders, wanting her to face him, to know he'd given this consideration.

That he cared what she thought of him. "I've been sending you mixed signals, and that hasn't been fair. It's also not what I want for us. I don't want the past between us. Hell, I don't want *anything* between us."

Her mouth parted in a little O. "That's ... sweet," she finally said.

"You're sweet." He pulled her toward him and covered her lips with his.

She gasped into his mouth, her hands coming up to grasp his forearms, and he braced himself for a hard shove away. Instead she curled her fingers, her nails digging into the fabric of his sweater. Her body softened, and she parted her lips, letting him in.

His tongue swirled with hers, the taste of her filling him, not just his taste buds but his heart. Which he had to admit frightened him. But he held on to the here and now, the feel of her in his arms, her fragrant scent arousing him beyond belief. His dick hardened in his jeans, being hard as a rock a feeling he was getting used to around her.

Her arms slid around his waist, and she tipped her head back, giving him deeper access to the depths of her mouth. She rose up on her toes, her kisses as ravenous for him as was his appetite for her.

*Woof.*

*Growl.*

*Woof.*

What started as an annoying sound ended with his big, hairy dog jumping on his hind legs, begging for attention from either adult.

She stepped back, laughing as she knelt to pet him.

"Fucking dog cock-blocked me," he muttered.

"Once again, he's doing me a favor. I really am here to conduct an interview," she said, cheeks flushed and whisker burn on her chin.

He opted not to mention it.

"That's the second part of my apology. You have free access to Lucas and Kade, along with Becky, my assistant. I know I was hesitant about this whole process, and I want to make it easy for you."

"Wow. You gave everything a lot of thought, didn't you?" she asked, sounding pleased.

"I gave everything about you thought." He grasped her hand, running a thumb over her soft skin. His emotions had shifted, and he had no choice but to accept it.

He had feelings for her that went beyond the sexual. In the short time he'd gotten to know her again, she'd taught him about forgiveness, caring, and moving forward.

"I appreciate that you listened." She leaned forward and kissed him full on the lips. "Now I need to get to work."

She walked out, hips swaying, and he watched, a big-ass grin on his face.

# Chapter Six

APPARENTLY CASSIE COULDN'T be around Derek without kissing him. Which, in turn, led to a stupid grin on her face, which would be unprofessional when dealing with his partners. She walked out of his office, relieved when his assistant wasn't at her desk. Cassie took a minute to compose herself. She placed her hands on her flushed cheeks and forced in calming streams of air.

Finally she felt ready to approach Kade, whose office Derek told her was in the far right corner of the floor.

She knocked on the door.

"Come in," he called out.

She drew a deep breath and walked into the room. A tall, dark-haired, broad-shouldered man stood behind an immaculate desk, clear of papers and clutter. Unlike Derek's which had been exactly what she'd expected of a busy business mogul.

"Hi, I'm Cassie Storms," she said, striding over and shaking his hand across his desk.

"Kade Barnes," he said rather formally. He gestured to an empty chair, and as she took her seat, he did the same.

She could tell by looking at him he wasn't comfortable with this meeting, and she thought she understood. Kade had been through his own PR nightmare, and he'd had to bare his soul on national television.

Now he had to talk to another reporter, even though it wasn't about himself. "I appreciate you taking the time to meet with me. I just want some insight into Derek in college. You and Lucas knew him best then."

Kade nodded. "We were all similar, actually. We came from environments where we didn't fit in, and when we met each other, we just clicked. A bunch of computer nerds who wanted to break out of their shells." He raised a shoulder, maybe in embarrassment, she couldn't be certain. Kade didn't show his emotions and was difficult to read.

"So you'd call Derek a nerd?" she asked with a smile. "We talked once the summer before college," she said, going back to that easy evening with a forbidden beer in her hand. "He didn't strike me as overly nerdy." He hadn't been as built as he was now, but he did have muscles from helping his dad work outside.

She bit down on her lower lip. "He was determined, even then," she mused, recalling how ready he was to go away to school. Just like she'd been.

"Definitely determined to succeed. Derek worked to pay for the extras above and beyond his scholarship. He was intent on making his parents proud. Especially his dad. Losing him took a toll."

"I'm sure. I know they were close."

"Right. You two have history," Kade said, studying her, making her feel like a specimen to be examined.

"Right." She refused to squirm. "Back to Derek's drive to succeed." She redirected Kade's focus.

"We all had that. But in those days, I think we were all less … secure in who we were. More easily used and hurt," he said, his words aimed directly at her, as was his fiery gaze.

"Aah. You're going there," she said, not surprised Kade knew her shared past with Derek, because the men were as close as brothers.

"I know you were a bitch," Kade said.

She flinched but accepted the verbal punch because it had been true. She had treated Derek badly. But she didn't plan to sit here and be insulted by his partner.

She rose to her feet. "I respect your honesty and how you're looking out for your friend, but did it occur to you that Derek can handle himself? Or that I might not be the same person today I was back then?"

He didn't answer.

"I didn't think so. It was nice to meet you. I think I've gotten a sense of what Derek was like and who he surrounds himself with." She turned and started for the door.

"Cassie, wait," he said, in a deep albeit reluctant voice.

She paused and glanced over her shoulder, hand on the doorknob. "Yes?"

"Derek's going to fucking kill me for being rude to you," he muttered. "Look, I'm sorry. I'm sure you know I've been through a rough patch lately. Someone I once trusted did his best to destroy me. It makes me wary about people coming back into someone's life. I questioned your motives and that wasn't fair."

She inclined her head, appreciating his apology and honesty. "If it makes you feel any better, I'm not looking to hurt Derek. In fact, I'm not looking for anything he doesn't want to willingly give."

"Good to know."

She squeezed the handle tighter. "Derek is lucky to have such a loyal friend."

"Right now, I'm not sure he'd agree with you,"

Kade said and Cassie laughed. "Our conversation will be our secret," she promised him.

He looked at her with what she hoped was appreciation in his gaze. At the very least, she saw a change from the wariness of earlier and she was grateful. Because Kade and Derek were close. And she wanted his friends to like her.

"Okay, on to the next adversary."

A few minutes later, she found herself sitting beside Lucas on a couch in the corner of his office. Another good-looking, dark-haired man, but this one with an easy smile on his face.

"So how's it going?" he asked her, reinforcing her impression that he was more relaxed than Kade, more like Derek in his demeanor.

"I'm having an interesting morning," she said, putting it mildly. "I met with Kade earlier and he's more intense."

Lucas burst out laughing. "Did he put you through the wringer?"

"You could say that. But I understood his reasons."

"We're protective of each other. We've been given good reason," he said, meeting her gaze.

She nodded. "I understand. And I'll tell you what I told Kade. I have no evil intentions toward your friend."

"Okay then. We can go on from there. So what can I tell you about Derek?" Lucas leaned back and grinned.

A little devil sat on her shoulder, and she heard herself asking, "Did he date a lot in college?"

"He was a player," Lucas said, and burst out laughing again. "No, seriously, he dated. I wouldn't say he worked his way through campus or anything. He was too busy working and studying. Then the idea of Blink came, and busy became an understatement."

Which reinforced her opinion of him as hardworking, dedicated, and ambitious. She and Lucas talked for a while longer, allowing Cassie to get a feel for their friendship, how they'd met, and how the deep bond between them developed and strengthened.

A knock sounded on the door and Derek walked in. "I'm going to steal her for lunch," he said just as they were wrapping up.

"We were finished anyway," Cassie said, rising to her feet. "Thank you. You were wonderful. I appreciate you taking the time to talk to me."

"My pleasure."

As they walked through the main area, passing the assistants and other people, she took in the vibe in the office, the relaxed feeling, the laughter, noting it for more information she'd reveal about Derek West's life.

Once they were in his office, he locked the door

and she knew she'd passed from the professional area into the personal one. A blanket was spread out on the floor beside the window overlooking the city. On it were assorted Chinese food boxes and bottles of water. A makeshift picnic for two.

"What's this?" she asked as she walked into the room.

"The last part of my apology and the first part of my seduction."

She nearly tripped over her own feet before righting herself. "Seduction?"

"You heard me." He swept his hands toward the setup on the floor. "But don't worry. I don't intend for our first time to be on the hard floor of my office. On the desk, once we're in a groove ... well, that can be arranged."

"Who are you and what have you done with Derek?" she asked the easygoing man with sex on the brain.

"Have a seat, let's eat, and we'll talk."

"Where's Oscar?"

"I had Becky take him back to my place and gave her the afternoon off."

"Aah." She kicked off her shoes and lifted her skirt until she was able to lower herself to the floor, her legs bent to the side. "Awkward," she muttered.

"Sorry. Guess I didn't take clothing into consideration," he said, his gaze zeroing in on the stretch of thigh she'd revealed. The lace on the top of her thigh-highs peeked out from the hem of her skirt.

"Quit staring," she muttered.

"Want to move things up to the desk?" he offered.

She shook her head. "No, this is nice. I'll manage. As long as you behave and keep your eyes where they belong." Because if she shifted even a little, her skirt would lift so high she'd be baring her underwear.

As it was, she was warm from his heated, knowing gaze; those very panties were damp with arousal. Because he'd used the word *seduction*. And talked about their first time, something she'd thought about too. Often.

The smell of delicious food caused her stomach to rumble, and he began to open the box tops. From dumplings to lo mein, fried rice to shredded beef, they shared a variety of dishes.

"So how did things go with Kade and Lucas?" he asked as he lifted the lo mein, more adept with chopsticks than she'd have thought.

"They were very enlightening. I understand you were a hard worker back in your college days."

"I had no choice. I needed to eat, so I needed to make money. And Blink was just an idea at the time, although one we were serious about creating."

She nodded. "Your mom must be proud of you,"

she said, pushing her boundaries with him—for good reason.

He swallowed hard but answered her quickly—and easily. "She is. She always believed in me, which I realize is a blessing not many people get from their parents," he said, meeting her gaze.

"No. That's true." She took a bite of the last dumpling, pausing to chew and swallow before continuing. "Speaking of family, I ran into my brother after you dropped me off at the house this weekend."

"Any chance he decided to leave you alone and let you stay in the guesthouse?" Derek asked.

She shook her head. "No, and I decided which apartment I want to move into. But we'll get to that, okay?"

He nodded.

"I'm going to bring something up that's bound to set you off. Except this time I want you to know I understand why."

He narrowed his gaze, obviously unsure of where she was headed with the conversation.

"Spencer wanted to know who dropped me off, and I told him it was you. He told me your mother stole a necklace and my father fired her. I didn't know. And I don't believe it."

She'd spent the weekend upset by the news. And no matter how many times she played out scenarios in her mind, she couldn't come up with one where she believed his mother would take something that wasn't hers.

Not the woman who had cookies and milk waiting for her in the kitchen after school—something the adult Cassie realized she must have wanted to do for her own son and daughter. But she'd had to work instead. Marie had been kind, caring, and giving. And Cassie considered herself a good judge of character.

Plus, she finally understood why Derek had such a difficult time putting the past behind them. Which meant it had to be discussed. Now, especially, that she knew he still wanted to be with her, despite their history.

Even if opening this dialogue led to more difficulties between her and Derek, she had to clear the air between them.

DEREK PAUSED, THE water bottle halfway to his lips, as Cassie's words bounced around in his brain. *I didn't know. And I don't believe it.*

He'd spent the weekend putting the past where it belonged, and she brought it up all over again. He searched for the words that would let him have this conversation and not be a jerk about her father or the past.

"Derek? I'm sorry to bring this up, but I thought you should know. My father told me your parents left and took new jobs. That's all I knew until I asked you the other day."

"What do you mean, you don't believe it?" He grasped on to the most unlikely part of the scenario.

"I know I was young, but your mother was so good to me. The woman I knew wouldn't steal. But … my father would lie. I just don't know why." Her wide-eyed, honest gaze met his, and he tumbled headlong into more than lust. This was the part of Cassie that called to him so deeply.

"I don't know what to say but thank you. I don't believe it either. I never did. I spent time with her this weekend. I guess I wanted to get her take on the past too. She's a lot like you. She's honest and she doesn't hold a grudge."

"I appreciate that," she murmured. "It's quite a compliment."

"I blamed your family for my father's death," he said, unable to meet her gaze, so he began to close up the empty food cartons as he spoke. "After they were fired, they had no health insurance. By the time he saw a doctor, it was too late to save him. I hated your father for that."

"And by extension, you hated me."

He shook his head. "No. I misunderstood who

you were, but we cleared that up pretty quickly. But the rest? I was shocked when my mother insisted she didn't feel the same way. Because my dad was stubborn, and there was no certainty he'd have seen a doctor anyway."

"She's forgiving," Cassie murmured. "And I'm so sorry about everything. I wish I could change it. At the very least, I wish I could give you answers as to why he accused Marie."

"I'm not sure it matters anymore." He'd felt lighter since leaving his mother's house and unburdening himself. He was able to talk about their past today without rancor.

"My mother had only good things to say about you," he told her.

She smiled at that.

"I take it your brother didn't have great things to say about me though?"

"I take the Fifth." She wriggled herself into a position where she could push herself up without flashing him in the process, and together they tossed the garbage into the trash can.

He decided to let the family issues go.

He lifted the blanket, folding it and placing it on the nearest chair. "So," he said, turning to face her.

"So." She leaned against the desk.

"Let's not discuss family."

"Good idea."

He stepped closer, backing her against the desktop, his pelvis coming into contact with hers. She sucked in a shaky breath. "I thought I was here to work."

"You are. You're shadowing me, remember?"

"I don't think I'll be writing about how you're trying to seduce your interviewer." A teasing smile lifted her lips.

He reached out and pressed his thumb against her lower lip, causing a full-body tremble. "Good. I'd hate to think you were the type to kiss and tell."

"I'm not." She swallowed hard, the long line of her throat moving up and down. "If you don't want something printed, it won't be. And I don't want anything personal between us up for public consumption."

"Fair enough," he said, bracing his arms on either side of her body and sliding his lips along her jaw. The scent of her perfume assaulted his senses, going straight to his cock, which hardened as if on command.

"Mmm. How do you do it?" she asked.

"What?" He worked his way up her jawline, enjoying the taste and scent of her as she arched into him, her breasts pushing against the sweater he now regretted wearing. He'd prefer to feel the press of her hardened nipples against a light tee shirt. Weather be damned.

"How do you engage my entire body with a simple kiss?" Her hands came to his waist. She pulled up the sweater, her hot palms touching his skin.

"It's us. This chemistry. It's unique to us." Mimicking her moves, he slid his hands inside her blouse, let his palms glide up her sides, until his thumbs grazed her nipples and she moaned out loud.

All he wanted to do was make her feel good. Watching her eyelids flutter closed, her lips part, the light flush cover her cheeks did something to him.

There was a reason he called her princess ... maybe the pedestal he'd put her on years ago. Maybe the fact that there was a vulnerability beneath the strength she exuded. Or maybe everything about her just did it for him. Which made him want to give to her.

He plucked at her nipples, and she tilted her head back, pushing her breasts forward and into his hands. They felt like a fucking gift, and he treated them that way, cupping the heavy mounds and continuing to roll her nipples between his thumb and forefinger. Her grip tightened on his hips. She liked what he was doing to her.

He intended to give her more. Add to the sensations. He eased a leg between her thighs, and soon she was rocking her pussy into the hard muscle of his thigh.

"Feel good?" he asked, continuing the nipple play. She was sensitive there, and for sure she felt the contractions deep in her sex.

"So good," she said, her body shaking and on the edge.

Fuck. His cock was hard, his balls had drawn up, and he wasn't the one who would be getting off from this. And that was okay. Another thing that made her unique. His desire for her pleasure over his own. Again.

He began to rock his thigh into the vee of her legs, and she rubbed herself against him, seeking harder, deeper pressure. He released her breasts, needing to kiss her. When she came, he wanted to taste her moans, to have his tongue tangled with hers, thrusting inside her mouth the way he couldn't do with her body.

His lips caught hers. At the same time, he shoved her skirt up and slid his hand into her soaked underwear, his fingertip finding her clit.

At the initial touch, her fingers pinched his flesh so hard he'd have bruises on his sides later, and he didn't care. He slicked her juices over the tight bud, and she came apart, her entire being a beautiful, quaking mess, her breaths lost in his kiss.

She rode out the waves, and he continued to slide his finger over her sensitive flesh until she was arching away from him, unable to take the sensations another minute.

When she collapsed against him, he was ready, taking her slight weight and pulling her into his arms. "You keep giving without taking in return," she said, her breath warm against his ear, her tone in utter awe.

What was wrong with the assholes who'd come before him? Not that he wanted to think about them, but she seemed truly stunned.

She reached for the button on his jeans, and he grasped her hand, stilling her before she could free his aching cock. If she so much as touched him, he'd come like a teenager first thing in the morning.

"But…"

"But nothing. Today was for you."

"And last time?" she asked, easing away so she could meet his gaze.

"Also about you. Remember what I said. I'm not about to fuck you for the first time on the floor or my desk."

He had a hunch he wasn't going to *fuck* her at all. Messy emotions were destined to make his life a hell of a lot more complicated. And he couldn't stop the feelings if his life depended upon it.

He stepped away, taking in her disheveled appearance. "C'mere."

She wrinkled her nose in confusion, and he leaned

forward to kiss her there. "Let's get you fixed up." He helped her tuck her blouse back into her skirt, and she smoothed her hands over the wrinkled material.

"My hair is a mess."

"It's fine," he assured her. "But let's smooth it out a little."

She blushed and began to run her fingers through the tangled strands.

He didn't think she'd want to do a walk of shame through his office so everyone looking would know what they were up to in here. Not that she'd have a choice. All the adjusting in the world wouldn't hide her flushed cheeks and well-kissed lips.

He snapped his fingers. "I have an idea." He headed to the phone on his desk and dialed Kade's office. "Do me a favor? Call a meeting of the assistants in your office." Those were the people who'd notice them walking to the elevators.

"Why?" Kade asked.

Derek rolled his eyes. "Don't ask me questions. Just keep everyone busy for a little while."

Cassie's lips parted in surprise. "Derek!"

He held up one finger, indicating she should wait.

"You're going to owe me," Kade muttered. "Tell me what to say to them."

"I don't know. Give 'em a raise. Or a Valentine's Day bonus."

Kade muttered a curse. "You're fucking crazy."

"I'd do it for you." He hung up the phone, turned to Cassie, and grinned. "We're leaving in five minutes."

"I look that bad?" she asked, horrified, her hands coming to her hair again.

"You're beautiful," he said, meaning it. "But you deserve better than to have everyone know what we've been doing."

She blinked, silenced at least for the second. "You're a true gentleman," she murmured.

He shook his head. "I'm not." At least, he hadn't been. She brought out the best in him. "Come back to my place?" he asked.

As far as he was concerned, they weren't finished. Not by a long shot.

"Okay."

# Chapter Seven

C ASSIE COULDN'T WAIT to get back to Derek's apartment and finish what they'd started. What he'd started and she intended to finish. Twice, she'd climaxed hard in his arms, and he'd expected nothing in return. She was desperate to feel him skin to skin, to give back and watch him come.

First they had to get past greeting Oscar. The dog, who she really thought was adorable, met her on his hind legs, begging for pets and kisses. She gave him plenty of each on his furry head before Derek excused himself to walk him.

Once she was alone in his apartment, she headed straight for the master bedroom, having already decided how she would welcome him when he returned. She kicked off her shoes, tucking them beneath the bench in front of the bed. She pulled off her blouse and laid it on the brown leather bench cushion, then gathered her courage and removed her bra. She moved on to her skirt and panties, folding them and placing them over the rest of her clothes.

A quick glance at the bed told her he wasn't a multi-pillow guy, so she merely folded down the comforter and settled herself into what she hoped was an alluring position, propping herself against the headboard, one knee bent. She waited, her nerves at an all-time high as the time ticked by slowly.

According to the clock, however, he took the dog for a short walk and returned quickly, hopefully because he was as eager to resume their activities as she was.

"Oscar, bed," she heard Derek say.

"Cass?" he called out, his footsteps growing closer, his deep voice causing her nipples to pucker into tight peaks.

She curled her fingers into the sheets. "In here," she replied.

He stepped into the room, shutting the door behind him. He leaned against the wooden frame, taking her in. His gaze slid from her face down to her chest, lingering on her bare breasts, her stomach, pausing at her sex before moving on down to her toes. When he finished his slow perusal, he worked his way upward again.

"Wow," he finally said, appreciation in his gaze.

The long stare gave her time for arousal to take hold, for her body to light up with sparks of need.

"You like?" she asked.

A sinful smile eased across his lips in reply. He lifted his sweater over his head, tossing it to the floor, revealing his broad, muscled chest. A light sprinkling of hair dusted his skin and traveled a path down into the waistband of his jeans, which he quickly removed, taking his underwear with them. One strong arm was tattooed, covered in a gorgeous sleeve, but her gaze quickly moved lower. At the first glance of his large erection, she swallowed hard, her entire body trembling with desire.

He wrapped a hand around his straining length and pumped his hand up and down the long shaft. A drop leaked out of the head, and it was all she could do not to moan out loud at the sight.

She patted the bed beside her. "Join me," she said, her skin tingling with the need for his touch.

"With pleasure." He strode over to her slowly, clearly more comfortable with his nudity than she was with hers.

He slid a hip on the bed, and then he was beside her, pulling her into his arms. His cock pressed insistently against her thigh, causing tremors of awareness to shoot through her body. The desire to feel him took hold, and she reached over, wrapping a hand around his cock.

He groaned at her touch. He was long and thick, and her sex contracted at the thought of him gliding fast and deep inside her. She took pleasure in the sleek feel of him gliding through her hands.

And when his mouth came down on hers, his tongue began to thrust and tangle with hers. She pumped her hand along his length in time to the momentum of the kiss. Her palm glided over the velvety-soft skin of his erection. Over the rigidness beneath. She couldn't wait to feel him thrust hard inside her.

With care, she slid her thumb over the sticky pre-come on the head of his cock, and he tore his mouth from hers, gasping for breath. "Damn. I don't know what's better. The feel of your hand or your mouth."

She grinned. "Decisions, decisions." She definitely wasn't used to having power, and she liked that she could cause this sexy, confident man to shake with need. For her.

He grasped both wrists and pushed her back against the pillow, throwing one leg over her waist and straddling her body with his stronger one. "You're teasing a man on the edge."

From the way his cock glided over her damp sex, leaking from the tip, he wasn't joking.

"Far be it from me to tease you." She lifted her

hips and rocked her pelvis against his, intending to tempt him further. Instead she was tormenting herself, need washing over her in unexpected waves.

He ground his hips into her body, and he felt so good, his hips pressing into hers. "Princess, you are killing me."

"But what a way to go, right?" she asked, her gaze holding on to his. And soon they were lost in another soul-touching, spell-binding kiss.

He gripped her wrists in his hands and rocked into her, simulating sex, his cock gliding over her clit, back and forth, over and over until she began the climb toward climax. Her body undulated beneath his, his erection rubbing against the exact right point of contact.

Pleasure took hold, her body quaking, on the precipice of ultimate gratification. "Oh God."

He released her hands and grasped his cock, gliding it over her sex hard, and she shattered, her climax rolling through her in delicious waves. She lost herself to sensation and his ability make her orgasm last.

And last.

Until she finally opened her eyes, small contractions still racking her body, to find him staring at her, a pleased look in his eyes. One that immediately turned hungry.

He obviously wasn't finished with her yet. He

rolled to the side and pulled open his nightstand drawer, producing a condom, which he deftly rolled on. And then he was over her again, the head of his erection poised at her slick entrance.

"Ready?" he asked.

She nodded.

"Then hold on because I've been dying to get inside you for too damn long."

He started gently, pressing into her, and she felt him, the head of his cock parting her sex, then filling her completely, pressing into her, inch by inch until he was as far as he could go. She gasped at his size, so big she felt him everywhere, and she arched up, her inner walls contracting around him.

"Derek," she whispered in awe as he lodged deep.

"I feel it, princess."

A perfect fit, she thought, and then she couldn't think at all because he began to thrust. In and out, faster and harder, and she raised her arms and grabbed on to the headboard, grounding herself.

He braced his hands on either side of her shoulders, arching his back, and he pounded into her. It was as if he'd been given the okay, and knowing she was braced and could handle it, he had the freedom to let go. Because she could handle him.

And she could. She wanted to. Every hard thrust took her higher. He altered his angle, bringing his cock into direct contact with a spot deep inside her she hadn't been familiar with until now.

"Derek," she said in awe as stars lit up behind her eyes and a harsh roar began to echo in her ears.

She wasn't inside her body anymore; she was part of something bigger than herself. Lost to sensation, only aware of his cock hitting that one glorious place, his big, damp body rocking over hers, his voice encouraging her to fly. And suddenly she did, peaking, screaming as she came harder, faster, and longer than she ever had before.

Her climax released his, and he came with a roar, his flesh slicked in sweat, his shoulders shaking, body trembling as he took her over the edge once more.

Time eluded her until finally he collapsed, but she hardly felt his weight, was barely aware of her surroundings. Her breaths came in short pants; her own skin was damp. She felt completely sated and wiped out.

After a time, she wondered if she'd passed out. It was as if all the years of waiting for him, which it felt like she'd done, and the current wondering of what could be between them had built up and exploded in a blinding flash. She curled her fingers into his shoulders, grounding herself in the reality of having Derek in her arms.

Without warning, he pushed himself off her and

headed for the bathroom. As she lay in his bed, the air around her cooling her skin, she listened to the sound of running water as he moved around the other room.

Finally he returned, standing beside the bed, arms folded as he stared down at her, an unreadable expression on his handsome face.

Self-conscious, she pushed herself up against the pillows, wondering what the protocol was here. It was the middle of the afternoon, but this wasn't her apartment. "Umm, I can go—"

"What? No." He sounded surprised she'd offer. "Why would you say that?"

She shrugged, her face heating. "You never know what the other person wants … after. You looked… I couldn't tell what you were thinking."

"I was just admiring you, in shock that we were together in my bed. After so long."

So his thoughts had mirrored hers, she thought with a smile. As if to silence her doubts, he dove onto the bed, smothering her body with his, kissing her until she was breathless again.

"I'm not going back to the office today," he said, settling himself on top of her. He held himself up enough not to crush her, but his heavy bottom half pressed into her pelvis, making her plenty aware of *him*. "In fact, I plan on spending the afternoon in bed. You?"

She laughed. "Well, considering I'm shadowing the billionaire tech god, I guess I'm staying in bed too. Although I don't want to make a habit of lounging around. I can't exactly write about the time you spend here in bed."

"Don't you think it's just as boring? My life isn't exactly titillating. I came from a poor background and I helped create an app that caught on. Big deal." He rolled to his side, wrapping himself around her.

She relaxed into him, and he played with her hair, sifting the strands beneath his fingers.

"I don't think your life is boring," she said. "Your background, how you accomplished your success… It's a big deal. People go to sleep at night and dream of winning the lottery. They make plans based on what they'd do with billions of dollars. You lived the American dream, and people want to know how you did it. That's exciting for them because they think if you can do it … so can they."

He groaned. "Well … when you put it that way, I understand the need for the interview a little more." She could tell he still wasn't comfortable with the idea.

"People are going to read, be fascinated by you. But there is an ironic part to all this." She breathed in the musky smell of his skin, her body automatically softening. Wanting him again.

"What's the ironic part?" he asked.

"Despite what people think, despite the sense that they want to be able to relate to you, to be you, the truth is, they can't replicate what you did. They only wish they could. You had the brains to create the app. You and your friends had the courage to act."

He smoothed a hand over her cheek. He cupped her jaw, turning her face toward him. "You're just flattering me so I'll do this thing. I already gave you my word."

She shook her head. "I'm serious. You are an example of preparation meeting opportunity. So even though I'll write the story, and people will dream as they read, they'll still know the truth. That you're special."

"You're biased." He brushed his lips over hers, distracting her from her mission of convincing him of his uniqueness, explaining why she wanted to write about him.

"No. I just see something special in you," she murmured. She always had.

When she'd hung out with him all those years ago by the pool, she'd seen something in him. Something that made her show up again the next night, even though she'd fully expected him to blast her with his anger after what she'd said about him.

Later, she'd watched his meteoric rise, all the while knowing he had that *it* factor. Brains, good looks, the right timing, and knowing how to capitalize on all of it.

All his partners possessed the same thing. Except in her eyes, Derek *was* beyond unique. He was loyal to his family, humble in ways she hadn't expected. He'd rocked her world in bed... And she was falling for him.

And though he hadn't kicked her out after sex, she didn't delude herself. Nothing good could come of them being together. They had too many outside obstacles working against them.

But that didn't stop them from being together now.

DEREK DIDN'T WANT to talk about himself. Not when he had a pliant, warm woman in his bed. Not when he could pick up where they'd left off. And his cock was ready to play again.

"Let's shower," he suggested, knowing full well they'd be doing a lot more than cleaning up in his oversized stall.

"Good idea. I can't stay too late. I have to take the train to the station where I left my car." She closed her eyes and groaned at the thought.

"You have got to move to the city," he said, already liking the feel of her in his bed. Of having her in his life. Around when he wanted to ... play.

"Speaking of moving," she said, her eyes lighting up. "I've decided which apartment I want to move into. The one on Eighty-Sixth street."

"Because it's closer to me. Good choice," he said smugly.

She rolled her eyes. "No, because it's larger than the others. It's going to be a big enough adjustment leaving a house for a one-bedroom. I might as well go big," she said, giving him a more rational explanation.

"Ouch. Way to deflate my ego." He liked his leap much better. But he'd enjoy having her close by, so he had no complaints. "I'll have Brad send you the lease agreement."

She nodded. "Thank you. I'd like to deal with this quickly. I don't want to take up too much time with the move. I'd rather have it be done and get on with my life, you know?"

"Whatever you need, let me know. I'm more than happy to help."

She blinked in surprise. "Well, that's nice of you. I'll keep it in mind." She leaned down and pressed a kiss to his chest, and his mind immediately stopped thinking about contracts and moves and moved on. "Now, about that shower?"

"I'm all for getting clean."

He swung his legs over the side of the bed, stood, and scooped her into his arms.

"Derek!" She kicked her legs, and he reached around, swatting her bare ass, causing another squeak. "Shower time, princess."

"You're bad."

"You like me that way. Come on." He strode to the bathroom and stood her on the rug before turning on the shower jets.

The heaviest spray came from the ceiling, but there were side jets as well as a handheld massager. Personally he wasn't interested in those. He waited until the water temperature heated before leading her into the steam-filled glass enclosure, shutting the door behind them.

"Let's start by getting you clean." He poured a generous amount of liquid soap into his hand and lathered up, then bent down and began to soap up her legs, working his way up her calves, massaging her muscles until she moaned out load.

The sound went straight to his cock, which now stood erect against his stomach. Ignoring the discomfort, he focused on Cassie, pressing his fingers behind her knees, moving upward along her thighs. Water sluiced down her skin, draining the soap away as he moved upward.

"Derek," she said, a warning tone in her voice.

"You're saying you don't want me to do this?" He used his thumbs, easing the pads along the seam of her thigh and her sex, slowly inching upward, pulling her outer lips apart.

"Ooh," she said, and as he glanced up, her head tipped up, her pure enjoyment clear.

"Step back, lean against the wall," he said, waiting until she complied. Once she was braced, he raised one leg and placed her foot on the small ledge where he kept the shampoo, exposing her for his view.

And his mouth and tongue. Then he licked her, from as far back as he could reach, along the seam of her inner lips, dipping inside, and ending at her clit, closing his lips over the tiny bud.

"Oh God."

He was sensing a theme. Her inability to speak more than guttural, pleasure-filled words. Which meant he was accomplishing his goal. He ran his tongue along her clit, teasing with soft flickers back and forth until she shook hard, her hands coming to rest on his shoulders. He eased her back with long laps, soothing her and letting the waves ebb before taking her up again.

"Fuck," she murmured, her nails digging into his skin, her sex arching, pushing at his face, her body pleading with him for harder suckling.

He had no problem complying. With his face pressing against her sex, she began to rock against him, and he gave her the pressure, the force she needed in order to break apart.

"Derek!" This time the scream was accompanied by a full-body climax, and he let her ride out the storm, drinking in her juices, her scent, her essence.

He rose to his feet, legs weak, when she met his gaze. "Fuck me. Now. Hard."

God, he wanted to. "Condoms in the bedroom."

She gripped his head in her hands, her eyes wild with need. "I'm clean. I haven't been with anyone in years."

"Me neither. And tested for life insurance." He bit the words out at the same time he lifted her up and slammed her down on his cock. He speared her with one thrust, and she cried out in pleasure.

"Yes. Yes." He drove into her, her back pressed hard against the stone tile, pummeling her with driving need.

His balls ached, drawing up, everything inside him on the edge.

"Coming. Now. Oh God, oh God."

He thrust again harder as she shattered, her orgasm a force that took him along with her, his entire body and mind consumed with pleasure.

He came back to himself to find a starry-eyed Cassie leaning against the wall, looking as sated as he felt.

He didn't know what the future had in store, but the here and now was pretty fucking great.

# Chapter Eight

OR THE NEXT two weeks, Cassie alternated between showing up at Derek's office and being at home, packing and moving into her new apartment. She'd hired a company to do the breakables, the things she didn't have to go through one by one. She chose what she wanted to furnish the apartment with and what she wanted to store, hopefully for a house in the future.

And during the process and the day of the actual move, she avoided her brother as best she could, her anger at him for displacing her growing instead of abating. For Cassie it was the principle of the thing, because she was beginning to look forward to living in Manhattan.

And she knew she had Derek to thank. She wanted to be closer to where he lived. To not have to rush out to take the train home after an intense sexual encounter, either in his office behind closed doors or at his apartment after work. She refused to think about what this thing between them meant, choosing instead to focus on enjoying what they shared. She'd never had a relationship that was easy, and this one was.

While at his work, she stayed in the background although she was always aware of Derek and their electric connection. As was he. He would always seek her out, his gaze falling on hers, no matter how busy he happened to be.

If he held a staff meeting, she'd be in the room, taking notes on how he handled his employees, but always aware of him. Of the authority he emanated, even if he was wearing jeans and a long-sleeve tee shirt. He didn't need a power suit to make his point. Because he was an easygoing and fair boss, his staff was loyal and appreciated him.

As for his daily routine, whether business ran smoothly or there was stress, Derek was calm under pressure. While Kade tended to blow up first and ease off later, Lucas and Derek were more mild-mannered. But all three men got the job done. They worked like a well-oiled team, and Cassie was impressed.

The day after her first night in her new apartment, she had lunch with Amanda, who she hadn't seen in a while, and then spent the afternoon at her office to catch up on what was going on and check in with her staff in person. Her second-in-command had been handling things while she was out on assignment, and he was happy to do it. She met with each of her writers, talked to the editors, and got a general feel for what had been happening in her absence, more than she'd been able to glean from phone calls.

When she'd decided to take over *Take a Byte*, the reporters and staff had embraced her because prior to her arrival, nobody cared what kind of magazine they put out. Morale had been low, rumblings of firings rampant. Cassie had insisted to her father that she wanted this project, and he'd agreed.

She realized now that he hadn't seen the inherent value in *Take a Byte* or how it could help rejuvenate the rest of the company. If he had, she'd be sitting in his old chair now, not her brother. She tried not to focus on what she'd lost; instead she promised herself she'd line up an impressive list of people after Derek and make her magazine one that the tech world turned to for information.

She was about to wrap up for the day when a knock sounded on her door. "Come in," she said without looking up from notes she'd been studying.

"So this is where you work."

She paused at the sound of Derek's voice, her stomach flipping happily at the sight of him.

"Hi! This is a nice surprise." She rose from her

seat.

"I had a meeting nearby, and since you said you'd be in your office, I decided to stop by and say hello." He stepped inside, a sexy grin on his face. "Actually I just missed you."

The flipping became outright cartwheels in her belly. "Well, welcome." She waved an arm around the comfortable-sized office.

He took it all in with one glance. It wasn't nearly as large as his, nor did it have the spectacular view, but she did have a window, and she had put homey touches around the room. A plant her mother had sent over, photographs of her family, pictures of herself and Amanda both when they were younger and abroad and more current ones.

He strode around the desk and pulled her into his arms, giving her a thorough kiss hello. His tongue swept over her lips before he delved deeper, sweeping inside and tasting her. She wrapped her arms around his waist. His jacket was cold from the outdoors, but she didn't care, pressing her body against his, the scent of his aftershave arousing her as always. It was a scent she'd forever associate with Derek.

He broke the kiss, then smiled, brushing her hair off her shoulder. "I was wondering if I could steal you for dinner after my meeting."

"You can." And maybe they could engage in some

catch-up sex, she thought, excited at the prospect.

He hadn't released her, his arms bracketing her body, and she rose to her tiptoes, about to kiss him again when someone cleared their throat.

She turned to see who'd entered without knocking, dismayed to see Spencer in the doorway.

"I thought this was a place of business," he said in that pompous-ass way he had of putting people down as he spoke.

Derek stiffened, and though she stepped back to deal with her brother, she slid her hand in his. A show of solidarity.

"Really? I thought it was *my* office."

A smirk edged his lips. One she recognized from when they were kids. He wasn't in a good mood, and they were about to do battle.

"I don't know why I'm surprised you're fooling around at work. It's not like you've been in the office the last week."

"Keeping tabs on me?"

"Cass, come on. I'm just aware of my employees' comings and goings."

She rolled her eyes, silently calling bullshit. Even away from the office, she knew more about what was going on than he did.

"What do you want?" she asked, losing patience.

Beside her, Derek rocked on the balls of his feet,

clearly ready for anything.

"I just thought I'd say hello. Aren't you going to introduce me to your ... friend?"

Oh, he knew exactly who Derek was, but she played along anyway. "Spencer, meet Derek West. Derek, this is my brother." She figured Derek needed no further explanation of who he was.

"I remember you," Spencer said, stepping closer. "The gardener and maid's kid."

"And proud of it," Derek said easily, but she sensed his leashed anger.

Understood it because it matched her own.

He didn't engage her brother in conversation or mention Blink or his current status in the world. Both men knew who Derek was today. Spencer was just trying to goad him. But Derek could handle himself, so she let the men deal with each other, stare each other down.

All the while she was seething inside.

The sound of Derek's cell phone finally broke into the charged silence. He glanced at the screen. "I have to take this. Excuse me." He shot her an apologetic glance and walked into the outer room.

"You're rude, Spencer."

"I'm honest."

She shook her head. "Not really, because you left a few important things out. Derek is the biggest news in the tech world. It was a coup to convince him to let me interview him, and that's where I've been. Out of the office. Working."

He frowned at the reminder. "Be that as it may, our family has a sordid history with his. I don't think it's appropriate for you to be interviewing him."

Or seeing him. Or fucking him. She could hear the thoughts rampaging through her brother's brain. The ones he at least had the smarts not to say.

She curled her fingers into fists at his ridiculous way of thinking. "Are you suggesting I turn my interview over to another editor or staff reporter?" she asked mildly, her blood boiling at the notion.

He shook his head. "I'm telling you not to do the story at all."

She flinched at his nerve. "You don't get to tell me how to run my magazine or what stories I can publish."

"I'm the chairman of the company." He smirked, and she wanted to smack the arrogant grin off his face.

"And I'm the executive editor of this magazine," she said, her voice rising. "Every story starts and ends with my approval. Unless you want me to take this decision to the board—and tell them you're denying me the chance to interview the billionaire tech god nobody else could get to even speak to them—I suggest you walk out that door right now."

His cheeks turned a bright red. She had him and he knew it. "This isn't over."

"What do you have against Derek, other than the fact that he made something of himself?" She really wanted to know. Spencer's feelings toward Derek made no sense, and she searched for an explanation.

"He's beneath us," Spencer said through gritted teeth.

The answer didn't work for her, but she knew she wouldn't be getting the truth out of him now.

Cassie shook her head and laughed. "If you ask me, Derek West is above us both. Good-bye, Spencer," she said, effectively dismissing her sibling.

"Cassie—"

"This discussion is over." She settled into her chair, picked up her pen, and glanced down at her notes, pretending to get back to work.

But the truth was, she couldn't see past the haze of anger that vibrated through her. Anger at how rudely he'd treated Derek, both to his face and behind his back. She was frustrated that she didn't understand his motivation for attempting to forbid her to interview Derek at all. Maybe it was jealousy, pure and simple. She'd probably never know.

Finally, the door slammed and she knew he was gone.

She breathed in deep, searching for calm, and was

still looking for Zen when Derek walked back into the room.

She wasn't sure how to face him after what her brother had said. She wouldn't blame him if he turned ice cold again or ended things between them altogether. There was just so much someone should have to take, and Cassie wouldn't blame Derek if he'd reached his limit.

Slowly she met his gaze, bracing herself for his reaction.

As far as Derek was concerned, Becky's phone call came just in time. He wasn't sure how much longer he'd have been able to stand in front of Spencer Storms and not go for the other man's throat. Derek was still on the phone with his assistant, wrapping up a problem, when the other man stormed out of Cassie's office, brushing past Derek without a word or a glance.

A few seconds later, he walked back into her office. He hadn't sufficiently calmed down—inside anyway—but he forced himself to remember *it wasn't her fault.*

"Hey. Everything okay?" she asked.

He nodded. "Becky had a few issues she needed me to address, and I need to head back right after my meeting. I'm going to have to cancel dinner."

Disappointment flashed across her pretty face. "Oh. Okay," she said. "I understand."

"Thank you." He shoved his hands into his pants pockets. "So, I saw your brother leave."

She nodded, her cheeks an embarrassed red. "I'm sorry about him. He's rude and unbearable."

"He's an asshole," Derek said bluntly. He didn't see the point in beating around the bush.

He'd promised not to treat her badly because of her family. He hadn't sworn to be nice to or about them. And Derek hated that smug bastard as much as he detested her father and what he'd done to Derek's mother. The fact that Spencer had had no problem reminding Derek of who he was, where he'd come from, and the vast differences between himself and Cassie only reinforced his dislike for the family in general.

He'd put Derek back in the frame of mind he'd been in before he'd promised Cassie he'd do better. Only his growing feelings for Cassie herself kept him from turning on her. He had to admit, it wasn't easy. That's how badly the son of a bitch got to him.

He propped a hip on her desk. "I can handle him," he assured her.

"I know. You just shouldn't have to."

"How about a change of subject? I have a fundraiser gala I have to attend this Saturday night, and I was wondering if you'd like to go with me. You'll get to spend time with my partners and their significant others. You can decide if that's a plus or a minus," he said, laughing, because the women in Kade's and Lucas's life were nosey and going to be damned curious about Derek and Cassie.

"Yes! Of course." Cassie's brown eyes lit up with pleasure. "I'd love to go," she said.

"Good. Now that you've agreed and can't get out of it, I should warn you there are long speeches, and it could get a little boring."

She rose to her feet, walked over, and placed her hands on his shoulders. Her warm scent enveloped him, and his cock grew hard. "How could I be bored when I'll be with you?"

Her reaction made him glad he'd asked. "I figured the night would give you more insight into my charitable contributions for your article."

She narrowed her gaze. "Umm, is this a date? Or am I going in my official capacity?" she asked, her arms sliding off his shoulders.

He grabbed her wrists and lifted her arms, wrapping them back around his neck where they belonged. "Guess."

She relaxed, the tension ebbing from her body. "I thought maybe my brother's behavior had changed your mind about whatever's going on between us."

He blew out a long breath. "I'll admit I had to do some serious talking to myself, but no. It's going to take more than your pompous jackass of a sibling to run me off."

A wide smile took hold. "Good to know you're a man of your word, Mr. West. So what is the event for?" she asked.

"The House of Hope. It's an organization that ensures no family suffers while a loved one is critically ill."

He'd been instrumental in its creation. From the time his father passed away, he'd wanted to do something for people in the position they'd been in. Families who couldn't afford to be with their loved ones because otherwise they couldn't keep a roof over their heads or food on the table.

Her eyes softened at his description of the organization that meant so much to him. "How so?" she asked. "How do they help?"

"If an adult patient is terminal, the organization steps in and helps pay—rent, utilities, food bills. Whatever is necessary. And they're currently raising money to build something akin to the Ronald McDonald Houses, or St. Jude's, where families can stay for free near hospitals."

"What a wonderful mission," she murmured, her

voice crackling with emotion. "I'm excited to attend and find out more about them. And just think about the all the people who will learn about it once your series of articles are published. People like you, with money, who want to donate to a good cause," she said, her enthusiasm rising along with his own.

"It'll give you added dimension, but the more important thing is the potential for raising money," she said with a bright smile.

It meant something to him that she understood the importance of House of Hope. Something that endeared her to him even more. There was so much they had in common, so much he liked about her, he thought, knowing he was falling and hard.

The problem was, they didn't live in a bubble, just the two of them. Her family existed, with all their flaws and issues. He'd dodged a bullet today, had been able to cope with her brother, probably because Becky's phone call had saved him from dealing with him for an extended period of time.

If the bastard had had time to continue, Derek might have ended up throwing the first punch and no doubt landing his ass in jail for assault if he'd even once mentioned Derek's mother.

He was only human, after all. And though he was doing his best to work around their problems, he didn't know whether they, as a couple, could ever get past the realities of life.

CASSIE SPENT HOURS getting ready for the gala. After doing some online research and talking to Derek again, she'd realized this was a black-tie event. Good thing she had appropriate dresses for the occasion. She was nervous to spend time with his partners and their significant others. She hoped the women were more like Lucas than Kade. She didn't want to have to fend off Derek's protective friends tonight.

He picked her up at her new apartment, and Derek West in a tuxedo was a sight to behold. His big body filled out his jacket, from his broad shoulders to his tapered waist. His hair was slicked back, and he presented a powerful figure, a sexy man who, tonight, was all hers.

"You clean up nicely," she said, her gaze drifting over him appreciatively.

"And you look fucking gorgeous." He lifted her hand, kissing the back before turning her around so he could get a three-hundred-and-sixty-degree view of her red dress.

The gown dipped low, revealing her cleavage in the front, while from behind, it revealed her lower back. It was the sexiest thing she owned, and she reveled in his blatant, admiring stare.

"Are you ready?" he asked.

She picked up her shawl and nodded. They traveled to the event by limousine, with a divider partition separating them from the driver. She sat by his side, her thigh touching his pants, sparks of awareness flooding her system.

He placed one hand on her bared knee, rubbing his thumb over the exposed skin. Her nipples were tight and her sex damp as they alighted from the car. It was destined to be a long night until they returned to her place, but she had something to look forward to.

Once inside, he led her over to where his friends stood. Nerves took flight in her stomach as he introduced her and, in the men's case, reintroduced her.

"Cassie, you remember Kade, and this is his wife, Lexie."

A pretty woman with brown hair and light blue eyes, in a silver dress, met her gaze with a welcoming smile. "Hi. Nice to meet you."

"Same here," Cassie murmured.

Derek placed a supportive hand on her back. "You already know Lucas, and this is his fiancée, Maxie."

A petite blonde with a slight baby bump leaned into Lucas's side, smiled. "Hi."

"Hello," Cassie said with a smile.

"And not to state the obvious," Derek said, "but this is Kendall, Lexie's—"

"Twin," the woman finished for Derek. "Hi."

"Hello." Cassie glanced between Lexie and Kendall, noting they were, indeed, identical. Both beautiful women, though Lexie's eyes sparkled with happiness, while it seemed Kendall was more subdued.

"And last but not least, this is Carter McCord, Kendall's date." He gestured to a nice-looking man with dark hair and a beard, who stood beside Kendall.

"Blind date," Kendall said with a brittle grin.

Cassie nodded, glad she wasn't in that position tonight.

"Derek, I'm really looking forward to walking Oscar. Can I come by to meet him tomorrow or another day this week?" Kendall asked. Her eyes lit up at the mention of Derek's dog.

"Sure. Let's do tomorrow. I only have another week left with my current girl. I'd love for him to meet you sooner rather than later. Just call or text me with a heads-up before you come."

"Great!"

"How many dogs do you walk at one time?" Cassie asked. Oscar seemed like enough of a handful.

Then again, she didn't own a dog, much as she'd love to someday. She didn't know how she'd handle more than one.

Kendall shrugged. "I don't do multiple families at once. So if one of my clients has two or three dogs, I walk them together. Otherwise just one at a time."

Before Cassie could reply, Kendall gasped, the color draining from her face.

"What's wrong?" Lexie asked, immediately coming to her sister's side.

"Julian's here," Kendall said on a horrified whisper, her gaze locked on someone across the room.

From her years covering the tech world, Cassie knew that Julian could only be Julian Dane, Lucas, Kade and Derek's former partner. The men had a sordid history that included a lawsuit and Julian staking a claim on Blink. He'd also tried to ruin Kade's reputation. Cassie didn't know what *Kendall's* issue with Julian Dane was, but the other woman was shaking.

"That son of a bitch," Kade muttered. "He knows this is something our whole team attends. I can't believe he'd show his face." His entire body turned rigid, and he took a step in Julian's direction.

Derek was faster, grabbing Kade and holding him back from confronting Julian and causing a scene.

"He's not getting near Kendall," Kade said, his anger tangible, clearly protective of his sister-in-law.

"Everyone breathe. I'll have him escorted out," Lucas said, heading across the room to avert trouble.

Kendall shook her head. "No. I'm an adult. I can handle being in the same room as him," she called after Lucas.

The other man ignored her.

Kendall started to go after him, but Lexie grabbed her hand. "Let Lucas handle it."

Kendall spun to face her twin. "I'm not sick. I'm stronger now and I know his game. I promise, you don't have to worry about me. None of you do."

Derek grasped Kendall's shoulders gently. "Kendall, it's not you we're all worried about, it's that snake. Why give him the opportunity to get close to you again?"

Kendall closed her eyes and sighed. "I'm just tired of everyone else fighting my battles."

He nodded in understanding. "I get it. But Kade considers you family, and he's protecting you the only way he knows how."

Cassie was taken in by Derek's gentle side, his delicate way of handling Kendall. Whatever the story behind Kendall's issues—*I'm not sick... I'm stronger now...*—Derek clearly understood how to make her feel empowered while diffusing the situation.

Lexie looked from her husband to her sister, obviously torn between them.

Cassie could help. "Kendall, do you want to get some breathing room?" she asked the other woman, because her date seemed utterly dazed and useless.

Kendall glanced across the room, where Lucas was talking to Julian, and a brief look of longing crossed her features before she turned back to Cassie. "Sure. I could use some freshening up."

Cassie turned to Derek. "I'll be back."

"Go," he said with a grateful smile. "I'll deal with things here and catch up with you soon."

Cassie and Kendall walked out a side door, nowhere near where Lucas and Julian stood. They entered the ladies' room, where they were luckily alone.

Kendall fell into the soft ottoman in front of the mirror and sighed. "I hate that one mistake keeps coming back to haunt me."

"You ... and Julian?" Cassie guessed.

Kendall nodded. "I'm bipolar. I was having issues and Julian took advantage. I had no idea he was using me to get to Kade. To help him get a part of Blink." Her lashes fluttered and a tear dripped from her eyes. She grabbed a tissue and blotted her face.

"You fell for him, didn't you?"

She swallowed hard. "We had a lot in common, or so he led me to believe. But he didn't know I was sick. And I wasn't ready to confide in him. I found out he was using me..." She shook her head. "I hate him."

Cassie wasn't so sure. Although he sounded like a class-A asshole, a part of Kendall clearly still had a soft spot for the man she thought he'd been.

"Let's change the subject," Kendall said. "What's

going on with you and Derek?"

Cassie laughed at the other woman's blunt honesty. "I'm not really sure."

"What about you? It doesn't look like you're thrilled with your blind date."

Kendall tipped her head back and laughed. "Now that is an understatement. We couldn't be more different. Looks like I'm in for a long night." She straightened her shoulders. "Might as well get back to it."

And since Cassie wanted to return to Derek, she agreed.

# Chapter Nine

W HILE DEREK WATCHED for Cassie's return, he hung with Lucas near the bar. Maxie had excused herself to take a phone call. He wasn't sure where Kade and Lexie had disappeared to, but Lexie was probably calming her husband down. Kade and the mere mention of Julian was an explosive combination.

Derek appreciated that Cassie had removed Kendall from the situation without knowing all the details. But now that Julian had left the event, everyone could get back to enjoying the evening. And he intended to do just that with Cassie when she returned.

"What happened with Julian?" Derek asked Lucas.

"What always happens with Julian. I read him the riot act, warned him to stay away from Kendall. He swore he didn't know she'd be here." Lucas shrugged. "I know we always come to the gala, but she doesn't.

So he could be telling the truth. But he couldn't take his gaze off Kendall either."

Derek groaned. "How's he doing?"

"He's mellower. Something's changed with him, though I can't put my finger on what. And since we'll never be tight again … I probably never will."

Derek let out a slow breath. "Got it. And agree. Listen, since I have you alone, I need a favor. Remember you hired a PI to look into Julian? I need the name of the company you used."

"Why? What's going on?"

Derek leaned an elbow against the wooden bar top. "I want to do some digging into Cassie's brother. Her old man handed him the chairmanship, and he treats her like shit. He spent the last year in Europe and has no business experience that I know of. I can't help but wonder if he's the weak link to my buying the company."

Lucas raised an eyebrow. "Interesting. The PI's name is Evan Mann. I'll text you the number tomorrow."

"Thanks."

"Are you sure you want to dig around behind Cassie's back?" Lucas asked.

Derek rubbed the back of his neck. "No, but I'm going to. My gut is telling me there's more to her brother than she knows."

Lucas leaned on the side of the bar with one elbow. "You know what's best. Are you still planning a takeover?"

Derek shook his head. "Not in a way that screws Cassie. I haven't figured out what I want to do, but information is my friend."

"She's coming." Lucas gestured toward the far side of the room, where Kendall and Cassie were walking toward them.

Kendall was attractive, but Derek only had eyes for the woman in red. Her dress had enough slits to tempt a man to sin, and Derek was more than ready to misbehave with Cassie, as soon as possible.

"Hi," Cassie said, joining him, a smile on her beautiful face.

Kendall waved and headed toward where her sister, Kade, and Kendall's date stood by a window across the room.

"I'm going to go find Maxie," Lucas said, excusing himself and walking away.

Derek turned to Cassie. "Hi, yourself. How is Kendall? Is she more settled?"

Cassie nodded. "She is, for now. But something tells me she and Julian Dane have unfinished business."

Derek frowned at that assessment. "That's not good. Because from what Lucas says, Julian doesn't seem finished with her. And I really don't want to have to bail Kade out of jail. He's extremely protective of his sister-in-law."

"Because of her mental illness?"

"She told you, did she?"

Cassie nodded. "I like Kendall."

"And that's why Kade is so protective. She's likeable. She's family and she's fragile, although less so by the day. And Kade can relate to someone having … issues."

"What aren't you saying?" Cassie asked.

Derek didn't normally talk about his friends behind their backs, but he trusted Cassie. "Kade deals with OCD and anxiety. He has a special affinity for Kendall."

"I see. But all is quiet for tonight?" she asked.

He nodded. "Want to check out the silent auction?"

"Sure." He clasped her hand in his, and they spent the next twenty minutes perusing the choices.

Every item, like seats behind home plate to a Yankee game, had a piece of paper with a starting bid and the increment in which bids could go up. All proceeds went to House of Hope.

Cassie paused at an item with a dog leash and collar on the table. Six months free dog walking, courtesy of Kendall Parker. "Oh!"

"Did you get a dog I don't know about?" he asked.

She shot him a wry glance and picked up a pen. Nobody else had bid yet. She scribbled her name, email, and a bid, then tried to pull him to the next item.

He held on tight to her hand and glanced down. "One thousand dollars for six months of dog walking, hmm? For a nonexistent dog?"

Her cheeks flushed pink. "You can use it for Oscar, and I'll have donated to an important cause. Now let's move on."

And he'd pay Kendall out of pocket, so she didn't lose out. Her donation was generous but he was sure she could use the money.

His heart warmed at Cassie's sweet gesture. Not only was she taking care of Oscar and, by extension, him, she was giving to his charity. Now he intended to bump up her bid and give even more.

He snatched the pen and scribbled his own information.

She glanced over his hand. "Five grand? Are you insane?" she asked, eyes wide.

"Why not? I can afford it and what better use than House of Hope? And don't you dare think of matching me. It's the thought that counts in this case, and I appreciate it." He tugged her close. "I appreciate you."

He slid a hand behind her, placed his palm on her

bare back, and pulled her against him for a kiss meant to express more than he was willing to say.

He traced the seam of her glossed lips with his tongue, slipping inside for a champagne-laced taste. "Mmm."

"Mmm is right." She tilted her head back and wiped the gloss off his face with her finger. "Red really isn't your color," she said with a grin.

"Maybe not, but it sure is yours."

"Why, thank you," she murmured.

Before he could dive back in for another taste, the lights above them flashed, indicating the cocktail portion of the evening was over.

"Ready to head over to the table?"

Cassie slipped her soft palm back into his. "Lead the way."

A few minutes later, they'd joined the rest of the group at the large table in the ballroom. Beautiful white flowers and gold lamé decorations sat in the center.

The speech part of the night began almost immediately. Derek normally tried not to fall asleep during these events, but tonight he had a captivating date. And he found a way to keep himself occupied.

He slid his hand beneath the long draping of the tablecloth that reached almost to the floor and began to pull Cassie's dress up, sliding his hand along the silken skin of her leg.

Her shocked gaze shot to his.

He kept his grin to a minimum but continued to play. Starting at her knee, he grazed her inner thigh with his fingertips, skimming his way up her flesh until she was visibly squirming beneath the table.

"Derek, stop," she whispered.

"Nope." He continued until his fingertips grazed the crease of her thigh and her sex, causing her to gasp, which she immediately covered with a light, deliberate cough.

"Are you okay?" Kendall asked from a few seats down.

"Fine." Cassie picked up a glass of water and took a long sip, forcing a smile. "See? All better."

He swiped his finger over her sex, finding her wearing a tiny thong. She moaned and clenched her jaw, shutting her mouth. He grinned and he slipped a finger beneath the damp fabric, finding her outer lips covered with arousal.

His cock throbbed against the placket of his pants, and he was grateful nobody could see either one of them.

"I'm going to kill you," she muttered, curling her hands into fists in her lap.

He placed his free hand behind her back and leaned closer. "Shh. Nobody is going to know." Back and forth he whisked, swiping her clit with each pass of the pad of his fingertip.

She trembled in her seat. He'd never been to a more interesting fundraiser, he thought, breathing in deep, inhaling her fragrant scent.

"And now we come to the honoree portion of the night," a new, louder voice at the podium said.

At least that meant the talking would be over fairly soon and they could move on to food. Which meant he could take her home and get her into bed.

He picked up the rhythm with his fingers, taking Cassie closer to the brink. She grabbed her napkin and held it over her mouth, faking a cough as her body began to shake and shudder beneath his hand. He let her ride out the orgasm, keeping an eye on his friends, certain everyone was involved in conversation with their own women. Nobody was paying attention to Derek and Cassie.

He brought her down, pulling her tighter against him. Finally, he removed his hand and pressed a kiss to her cheek. "Should I apologize?" he whispered in her ear.

"Don't say another word." She placed the napkin back in her lap. Her cheeks were pink, her eyes glazed.

"Hey. Derek." Lucas punched him in the arm, just as everyone in the room began to clap. "That's you. Get up there."

Payback was a bitch. He now had to face the crowd, the people looking at him expectantly. All of which was enough to kill his erection.

Still, he took his time acknowledging Lucas's words. Accepting congratulations around the table. And reveling in Cassie's kiss before rising to his feet to accept his award for the work he'd done and the money he'd donated to House of Hope.

CASSIE INVITED DEREK to sleep at her new apartment for the first time, and the same limousine that had dropped them off took them there. He called a neighbor to feed and walk Oscar, both tonight and in the morning, and he was all set.

They arrived at her place and left their coats in the front hall. They kicked off their shoes before making their way to the bedroom.

"I'm so proud of you," she said, unhooking her bracelet and placing it on the nightstand. "Congratulations on being honored tonight. I can't believe they surprised you like that."

Cassie tried not to think about what *she'd* been doing seconds before his name was announced. *As* his name was announced.

"Thanks," he said, not meeting her gaze. He'd been humble about it since his acceptance speech, which had brought a lump to her throat.

*My parents had no insurance when my father became sick. If my mother hadn't had to work two jobs to put food on the table and to pay rent, she would have had more time with my father at the end. I want to make sure other families have the time my parents didn't.*

Cassie's heart had hurt listening to his words. Her family had the money to make sure their employees had insurance. They could have given Marie time off to be with her husband. Instead she'd already been fired, accused of stealing. It still didn't make any sense to Cassie. She definitely planned on talking to her mother about it next time they were alone together. She wanted her mom's take on what had happened. And why.

"House of Hope is lucky to have you," she told him.

"It's just something I need to do," he said, placing the plaque he'd been given on her dresser top.

He shrugged out of his jacket and laid it over the vanity chair in the corner.

She strode over to him on bare feet and met his gaze. "Well, this is something *I* need to do." She reached up and unhooked his bow tie, tossing it to the floor.

Next she worked the buttons on his dress shirt, unhooking them one at a time, revealing his bare chest, a light sprinkling of hair, and the hard muscles that tapered into his slacks. She slid the shirt off his shoulders, letting her hands trace the strength in his upper arms and chest before dropping the garment to the floor too.

Unable to resist, she leaned in and breathed in the scent of him, his cologne and raw masculinity, tracing the tattoo along his left arm with her mouth.

"So sexy," she murmured, trailing her lips along the black ink.

His big body trembled. "All this because I won an award of some kind?" His lips twitched in amusement.

"No, all this because you're you." She ran her tongue across his chest, around first one nipple then the next, tracing the same path with her fingertips.

She undid his pants, hooking her thumbs into his briefs, and pulled both down. He kicked them off, and then he stood before her nude. Exactly the way she wanted him. Naked and erect, there for her to do whatever she desired.

She lowered herself to her knees, and he groaned at the implication of her pose. She had no intention of disappointing him. He spread his legs, bracing his weight, and she grasped his shaft in her hands.

He slid his hands into her hair, messing up her blow-dry, not that she cared. He gripped the long strands just as she cupped his balls in her hand and drew his cock into her mouth, swirling her tongue around the rigid length.

His grip tightened, pulling at her scalp until her eyes watered. She accepted the pain, a good hurt that reverberated inside her body, all the way down to her sex. Giving to him turned her on.

Who knew? She wasn't an expert. This wasn't something she made a habit of doing with guys, mostly because her experience had been with quick sex. Nothing with Derek was typical, and no matter what happened, she had memories to last a lifetime. Right now she wanted to make sure she made an impression on him so he'd never forget what they'd shared.

She held the base of his cock in her hand and began to suck his shaft, pumping her hand up and down at the same time.

"Fuck, princess. You feel good."

She smiled around his thickness and kept up her movements, aware of how quickly he was closing in on coming by his harsh grip in her hair, the way he began to thrust into her mouth. The head hit the back of her throat, and she managed to swallow around him, causing a harsh groan from him.

"Damn, I'm going to come," he warned her.

She refused to back off, wanting to take him all the way. Her own arousal was off the charts, her panties wet, her sex full and pulsing with need.

He thrust into her mouth, once, twice, and came with a loud groan, and she swallowed everything he had to give.

She was about to collapse onto the floor when he lifted her up and carried her to the bed, coming down beside her. He propped himself on one side and curled her hair around his hand, and they lay together, their breathing synchronized, the world around them quiet.

She could get used to this, she mused, happy with a man for the first time. That the man was Derek continued to take her by surprise. But the more time they spent together, the more she fell under his spell.

DEREK CAUGHT HIS breath, well satisfied after the surprise blow job she had had given him. She never ceased to amaze him. From how kind she'd been to Kendall, a woman she'd just met, to the generous donation she'd been willing to make to House of Hope, to watching her drop to her knees in front of him…

He'd never been so fucking hard … or humbled in his life. There was something special about this woman, something he'd known from the first, all those years ago.

She had him wrapped around her pretty little finger. Not that he had a clue what to do with her.

"Question," he said. Because Lucas had reminded him he was getting married next weekend in a small ceremony, and after seeing him with Cassie tonight, he'd offered to have Derek bring her as his date.

"Yes?"

"Maxie and Lucas are getting married next weekend. On Valentine's Day."

"Aww, that's so romantic."

He smiled at that. "Do you want to come as my date?"

"I'd love to! Thank you." She leaned over and placed a kiss on his chest, and his body stirred. It didn't take much when it came to Cassie.

"I had a nice time with everyone tonight," she said. "Lexie, Maxie, and Kendall were sweet."

"Glad you liked them. They're all good people."

"Not Julian?" she asked.

He paused. "Julian *was* a good guy. He was one of us. And then he got involved with the wrong people. Drugs... I wouldn't have thought he was capable of the shit he pulled on Kade, but I guess I didn't know him as well as I thought." But Derek had a problem thinking of Julian as all bad.

"I think something had to have happened for him to do what he did to someone he once considered a friend." Derek shook his head. "But I don't know."

"Kendall seemed upset to see him. But she

couldn't stop staring at him either."

Derek frowned. "That went both ways. But if she knows what's good for her, she'll steer clear. Kade will never forgive him, and she needs her twin on her side."

Cassie sighed. "Family is complicated. Relationships are complicated," she mused.

"Life is fucking complicated."

Her laugh warmed him. And his groin started to perk back up again. He pushed himself up and rolled on top of her, his now hard cock gliding over her soft, wet pussy.

He brushed her hair off her face, staring into wide brown eyes at the same time he raised his hips and pushed inside her, gliding home as if he belonged there.

They groaned in unison, their joining electric.

He rolled his hips against hers. He kissed her, sliding his lips back and forth, losing himself inside her. She grabbed his hair in her hands, holding him tight as they rocked together, climaxing simultaneously, his entire being caught up in hers.

They lay in silence, his eyes growing heavy.

Derek woke to the smell of something delicious cooking. With a grin on his face, he headed to the bathroom, used her toothbrush, and washed up before he met her in the kitchen.

"Something smells good."

She placed a plate on the table, then turned to face him, wearing a long tee shirt, her bare legs peeking out, and a bright smile on her face. "Morning." She settled into the chair at her small table.

"Morning."

"Have a seat and dig in." She gestured to the pancakes and orange juice at his place setting.

He happily complied, inhaling the warm scent. "I can't remember the last home-cooked breakfast I had."

"You've been deprived. I'll have to make it up to you." She winked and began cutting into her breakfast. "I'm starving."

"Because you worked up an appetite last night."

Her gaze shot to his, her cheeks flushing, her eyes darkening at the memory. "Yes, I did."

They paused to eat, him smothering his with maple syrup. The food was as fantastic as the aroma. "You're a good cook."

"Thank you." She placed her fork down and met his gaze. "So I need to talk to you about something."

"Go ahead."

She shook her head. "It's a touchy subject for you."

He narrowed his gaze. "Okay…"

"I've been collecting a lot of good information for

the kind of article I want to run. I can delve deep into your college years, the creation of Blink, and how you run the company. I've even got your charitable contributions down too. But…" She paused to lift her glass and take a sip of juice. "Something's missing," she said, placing the cup on the table.

An uneasy feeling settled in the pit of his stomach. "And what would that be?"

"Your childhood," she said bluntly. "I'd like your permission for me to call some of your old teachers, and I'd like to meet with your mother and sister," she said on a long breath.

She was right. It was touchy. His initial, gut instinct screamed a loud *no*. Of course, she could call teachers without asking him, so he appreciated the fact that she'd asked him first. But that wasn't the sensitive part of her request.

His mother.

His sister could handle a conversation with Cassie. Brenda was married and had a two-year-old daughter. She'd always been a straight shooter, and Derek didn't have an issue there.

"Derek?" Cassie broke into his thoughts. "I'm not going to upset her. I won't ask about the circumstances of her leaving my parents' employ. I just want to know about you as a kid."

He understood why she needed to do it, and he

understood that if he said no, he was ruining any further chances between them. She'd forgiven him each time he'd been an outright asshole because she'd mentioned his parents or the status differences between their families had come up. But she'd flat out told him to get over it or walk away.

Which meant it all came down to trust. Did he trust Cassie not to bring up the touchy parts of his mother's past? Yes. He did. Was he ready for her to talk to his mother, to have those two parts of his life come together?

"Okay," he said, surprising even himself at how quickly he'd answered those internal questions.

Her eyes opened wide. She obviously hadn't expected such a fast or simple answer. "Thank you." She jumped up, coming around to his side of the table to wrap her arms around his neck and give him a hug. "I know how difficult it was for you to agree to. And I appreciate your faith in me. I really do."

He breathed in her scent, allowing her nearness to calm his rapidly beating heart. Because no matter how much he trusted Cassie, allowing anyone to ask questions and dig into the most personal parts of his life just wasn't comfortable.

"I'll need to talk to my mother, give her a heads-up, and set it up," he said as Cassie untangled herself from him.

"Whenever you're ready," she assured him.

He blew out a shaky breath. Though he knew his mother would be happy to meet with Cassie, Derek still needed time to prepare himself. Because allowing the two women he was closest to to meet spoke more about his feelings for Cassie than he was ready or willing to admit.

# Chapter Ten

L ATER IN THE week, Cassie waited at her mother's favorite restaurant in Manhattan. In between going to her own office, writing some catch-up articles, and shadowing Derek when he had different things on his agenda for her to see—meetings with developers and investors he didn't mind her sitting in on as long as she signed a confidentiality agreement on the details—she called her mother and asked her to meet for lunch.

No doubt about it, Daniella Storms was a stunning woman. Heads turned when she walked into a room, a combination of the confidence with which she carried herself and her outer beauty. She wore a fur jacket, real not fake because she didn't care about being politically or morally correct, a pair of navy wool slacks, and a turtleneck, with a patterned scarf around her neck.

The hostess escorted her mother to the table, and

Cassie waved as her mother rushed over to meet her. "Cassandra, I've missed you," her mom said, greeting her with a kiss on the cheek.

"I haven't been gone that long, but I miss you too." For all her mother's faults, which stemmed from having too much money and not enough self-awareness, Cassie had always felt her love.

"I'm glad you asked to have lunch but I'm surprised. You usually don't have time during the workweek." Her mother put her jacket next to her in the booth, loath to have it checked and possibly lost.

"I know. I wanted to talk, but let's catch up and order first, okay?" Cassie didn't want to start their meal with a conversation that might cast a pall over their time together.

Cassie was starving and decided to splurge on her food, ordering fettuccini Alfredo and a Diet Coke. Her mom ordered a Niçoise salad and a glass of Chablis.

Her mother talked about her charities and the work she'd been overseeing. Cassie mentioned her in-depth interview but deliberately avoided revealing with whom, saving that information for their talk later.

Since her mother didn't bring up Derek's name, Cassie assumed Spencer hadn't ratted her out to her parents. He might not like her being with Derek, but he wasn't doing anything to prevent it either. At least not yet.

"So what did you want to talk about?" her mother finally asked over coffee.

Cassie wrapped her hands around the warm cup. "You know the interview I mentioned earlier? What I didn't say was that the subject is Derek West." Cassie dropped his name and studied her mother's face.

Her mother wrinkled her forehead in thought, as best she could with all the Botox she'd had. "Derek West," she repeated. "Is that the son of Marie and Thomas West? They worked for us when you were younger," she said, no hint of bitterness or anger in her tone.

"Yes, Mom. That's him. He's a brilliant tech developer, and frankly he's worth billions now."

Her mother's eyes opened wide. "Well. That's really something. Good for him," she said over a sip of her coffee.

"Mom, why did his parents leave?"

Her mother paused in thought. "As I recall, they left to work for a family who had a home on the water, in the Hamptons. Why?"

That was the story Cassie knew from her father. "Did Marie or Thomas tell you that themselves?" she asked.

"No. I was away at a spa week with your aunt Mary and a friend. It was an annual trip we took. When I got home, your father told me they had quit.

We went through quite the trial trying to replace them, as I recall." She narrowed her gaze. "Why all the questions?"

Cassie swallowed hard, then leaned forward on the table. "Well, Derek said they were fired. In fact, he told me that they were let go with no warning. They lost their health insurance and were given no references. Soon after, Thomas got very sick. By the time he saw a doctor, it was too late."

"No. That's not possible. We always gave our help a nice severance and letter of recommendation. And I know I would have done that for Marie. She worked for us for years. She took such good care of you."

"Derek said Dad accused her of stealing family jewelry."

"What? No. Marie wouldn't steal," her mother said emphatically.

"That's how I feel."

Her mother rubbed at her temple with one hand. "But that would mean your father lied to me."

"And to me as well," Cassie said. "He told me the same thing when I came home on a break and the Wests were gone."

Marie studied her nails, deep in thought. "That's a terrible accusation to make about your father."

Except her mother never really viewed her father in a realistic light. She saw what she wanted to see, what made it easier for her to live with him.

Cassie decided to take this from another angle. "Let's look at it this way. Why would Derek make up such a tale? I saw his pain. He lost his father and feels responsible because he didn't have the money to help him then. He gives to a charity that pays for working people to take time off to be with their loved ones while they're sick." Cassie drew a deep breath. "I believe him. Which means I can't ... don't believe Dad."

She had no choice but to put the final piece of the puzzle in place. "Spencer saw Derek drop me off at the house one day. He was furious. He said Derek was beneath me and that his mother was a thief."

Her mother met her gaze, eyes shimmering, taking Cassie off guard with the unexpected show of emotion. "I know your father doesn't always play by the rules. He's self-absorbed. He makes excuses for your brother. But what you're saying would mean he deliberately destroyed people's lives."

Cassie reached across the table and grasped her mother's hand. "I'm sorry."

She looked at Cassie, sorrow in her eyes and expression. "In a marriage or relationship, you overlook a lot."

Cassie refused to believe that. In her mother's marriage, she chose to disregard many signs that would paint her father in a negative light.

Her choice.

Her life.

Not the way Cassie would opt to live her own.

She gathered her thoughts and her courage. "No, Mom. I think it's the way you decided to live. So you could go on being married to Dad. I'm not judging you, but people were hurt. Very badly hurt." She shook her head. "I don't know that I can forgive that."

Her mother dabbed at her eyes. "I hope you never have to make difficult choices," she murmured. "I need to go."

Cassie rose to her feet. She rushed over and pulled her mother into a hug. "I'm sorry to be the bearer of such difficult news."

"Maybe there's an explanation," her mother predictably said.

"Maybe," Cassie said.

But she highly doubted it.

DEREK WORKED LATE thanks to a server crash that had them in a panic for most of the day. Kendall had met Oscar, they'd hit it off, and she'd started walking him the next day. He called her to give him an extra walk today, which she'd done with no problem. He was glad his pup was in good hands, which took the pressure off of him on what time he had to be home.

He was ready to shut down his computer and head home for the day when his cell rang. A glance at the screen told him it was Evan Mann, the private investigator he'd hired a few days ago.

"Hello?" Derek said.

"Mr. West, Evan Mann. Is this a good time to talk?

"It is."

"I did some digging, although to be honest with you, it didn't take much. Spencer Storms doesn't bother to cover his tracks."

Derek narrowed his gaze. "What did you find?"

"Your boy likes to scam women. Left a trail of broken hearts and empty wallets wherever he went. And the women were all too happy to talk about him and what he stole from them."

"Interesting."

"Now, back home, that's another story. And since I can't believe he only behaves that way abroad, I'm guessing he covers his tracks better in the United States. That's what I've got for you so far. In a nutshell. Details to follow in a report. Want me to keep digging?" he asked, speaking in his gravelly voice.

Derek picked up a pen and tapped it against the desk. "Keep looking. And thanks."

Derek leaned back in thought. Something was bothering him about Cassie's brother, but he couldn't put his finger on what. So he pushed it aside, knowing it would come to him when the time was right.

He shut down his desktop just as Lucas walked into the room.

"Hey," Derek said, bracing his hands behind his head and leaning back in his chair. "Long fucking day."

"No kidding." Lucas dropped into the chair across from Derek's desk. "When technology works, it's brilliant. When it fails…"

"Epic pain in the ass." Derek grinned. "Well, it's all sorted out now. So. Are you ready to get married?"

It was Lucas's turn to push back and brace his hands behind his head in a relaxed, happy state. "I can't wait."

"Good. I'm happy for you."

"Thank you." Lucas grinned.

"So I just heard from the PI."

"Really. What'd he find?"

Derek filled Lucas in on Spencer's history of fleecing women. "I feel like there should be warning bells going off, but I can't figure out what I'm missing."

Lucas grunted. "You'll figure it out. Do you know what you're hoping to find?"

"Damned if I know. Right now I'm just following my gut. But if I can find anything that becomes an issue with him running the company, even better."

"So you can take over?" Lucas leaned forward in his chair.

"Maybe." Or so Cassie could.

Derek knew how much that opportunity meant to her. How badly she wanted to save her grandfather's company and make him proud. The better he got to know her, the more time he spent with her, the more he wanted that for her too.

Lucas studied him. "You're softening. Because of Cassie."

"Maybe I am."

"She's good for you, then. I like seeing you happy," his friend said.

"Can't say I mind it myself." Derek's phone buzzed with a text message.

*Miss me?* It was Cassie.

*Always,* he wrote back. Which, he was surprised to realize, was true.

*Your place so Oscar isn't alone?*

Leave it to her to worry about his pet, he thought, feeling a grin on his face.

"I take it that's her?" Lucas asked.

Derek had all but forgotten he was in the room.

"Yeah." He typed back, suddenly eager to see her.

*You. Me. Naked. Make my long day a distant memory.*

*Be there soon,* she wrote back immediately.

*On my way.* "Gotta go," he said to Lucas.

Lucas pushed himself to standing. "Far be it from me to keep you from getting laid."

"Fuck off," Derek muttered with a grin.

"Bye." Lucas strode off, laughing.

Derek rose and grabbed his jacket from behind the door, in a rush to get home. Because he needed her, he realized. Needed her to help him unwind after a shitty day, needed her for peace of mind and for the best sex he'd ever had.

Because it wasn't just sex. That was something he'd realized the last time they were together. It wasn't sex anymore. It was making love. Something he'd never experienced before, which made it both easy to recognize as different and scary as fuck.

Although they hadn't been together long, he felt like he'd always known her. That they shared a connection that went back in time and transcended misunderstandings in the past ... but not socioeconomic differences.

How could he be in love with the girl in the mansion across the way? Never mind that now he was the one with the money to buy as many mansions as he wanted, in whatever country or on whichever island he chose. There was still that class difference.

Her family didn't approve of him. At least her brother didn't, and he knew damn well her father would hit the roof. He didn't know about her mother, but he had his doubts she'd take her own stand in her daughter's favor.

When it came down to actually choosing, if it came down to that, could Cassie walk away from her family? Would they make her opt between them?

Could Derek put her in that position?

Fuck. Well, no decisions had to be made now. He was going home to have more fantastic sex with the girl he couldn't get out of his head or his heart. He'd worry about the other issues as they arose.

Because he wasn't giving her up without a fight.

He didn't hit traffic on the highway and arrived home in near record time. Oscar greeted him, and he beat Cassie here because, though his doorman had instructions to let her in to his apartment, the rest of the place was dark.

He flicked on the light just as the knock sounded on his door. He let her in and allowed for Oscar's crazy-boy greeting, knowing he'd never get the dog to settle if he didn't have his licks, pets, and hellos.

She knelt, her big down parka dragging on the floor as Oscar did this thing. Cassie giggled and crooned to him before Derek called him off. "Oscar, come on, boy. Come here. Bed." He walked to the kitchen and returned with a high-value treat that would keep him occupied for a good long time.

Then he turned to Cassie. "Hi."

"Hi."

He took three steps forward and pulled her into his arms, sealing his lips over hers. The kiss immediately turned hot, this despite the fact that she wore a puffy jacket and there were barriers of clothing between them. He bit her lower lip and she moaned into his mouth, his tongue sweeping through, tasting her, devouring as best he could.

Needing to feel her skin, he pulled back, unzipping her jacket and tossing it to the floor in the hallway. She kicked off her shoes.

"Do I need to feed you dinner first?" he asked, trying to be a gentleman.

"No. Just hungry for you."

Apparently they were on the same page. "Bedroom. Now."

Her eyes darkened with agreement and desire. Not long after, they were naked and in his bed. He pulled her against him. Her hands were cold from the outdoors. But her body was warm, her skin flush against his, her scent permeating his nostrils, the familiar, arousing aroma of her shampoo filling his senses in all the best possible ways.

Maybe it was because he'd let himself admit, at least to himself, that he was falling in love with her. He wasn't ready to speak the words aloud, but the way they came together, their bodies meshing, their minds in sync, he didn't have to right now. He just needed to feel. Just wanted *her* to experience the same emotions rushing through him right now.

He kissed her lips, all the while trailing his hand down from her throat to her chest, cupping her full breasts in his hands. She arched her back, pressing the mounds into his hands, all but begging him to grip her harder.

His cock throbbed hot and hard against her thigh, but he pushed back his desires, wanting to taste her, to savor her body before getting to the main event. He held one soft mound in his hand, bent his head, and pulled her taut nipple into his mouth, suckling on the bud until she was writhing beneath him, gripping his hair in her hands.

He swallowed a groan and slipped one hand between her thighs, cupping her sex. She was damp and ready for him as he slid one finger inside her, gliding in and out, her slick muscles gripping him tight. He trailed his mouth down over her breast, lower to her belly, pausing to lick at her belly button before following a trail down to her sweet pussy.

He dipped his head and pressed a kiss against the top of her mound, sliding his mouth along her outer lips before licking her clit.

"Oh God." She raised her hips, and he sucked at the tiny nub, pulling it between his teeth, nipping, then soothing with longer laps of his tongue. "Derek," she groaned.

The sound went straight to his dick, and he pulsed harder, wetness trickling against her leg. One orgasm, he promised himself. He'd give her one climax and he'd bury himself balls deep inside her.

He pumped his finger inside her, curling it against her fleshy inner walls, and she started to shake. He continued to lick at her clit, around, over, back and forth, alternating sensation and pressure, all the while continuing to massage that sponge-like spot inside her.

She arched and gripped his head once more, holding him in pace as she moaned through her release, his name on her lips. He continued to lap at her gently, bringing her down, until she released his hair and collapsed back against the bed.

He moved over her then, grasping her hands and drawing them up over her head. At the same time, he aligned his cock at her entrance and slid home.

"Derek." Her eyes opened wide as he settled between her thighs, thick and hard inside her.

"Hey, princess." He grinned at the glazed look on her face. He pulled out and glided back in once more, pressing hard enough for her to feel him deep.

"Again?" she asked, dazed and surprised.

He wasn't. Together they were electric.

"Feel me?" he asked her.

She whimpered. "Everywhere."

"Good." He picked up his pace, aware of every nuance in her expression, telling him which shift of his hips gave her pleasure, which didn't provide enough pressure, how to move to please her even more.

And as he thrust in and out, it was all about pleasing her, holding himself back, ignoring the ache in his balls, the need to come hard. When she started to shudder beneath him, he let go, pumping his hips and taking them both over the edge. He detonated inside her, his entire body caught up in the explosion. His ears rang, white bursts of light flashed behind his eyes, and he came harder than he ever had before.

When he came back to himself, he felt Cassie's fingers sifting through his hair, a delicious ending to a perfect moment.

"I'm crushing you." He pushed himself up and rolled off her.

"Don't go far," she murmured, sounding as wiped out as he felt.

"I won't." He pushed himself back against the pillow, pulling her into him. "You okay?" he asked.

"Perfect." She placed a hand on his chest and yawned. "But I have to say you can feed me now."

He laughed. "I think I can manage that. What are you in the mood for?"

"Chinese? Pizza? Sushi? I'm easy."

"Sushi works." He walked to his pants and pulled out his cell phone from the pocket, then came back to bed. They opened the delivery app and ordered.

"What did you do today?" he asked her.

"Umm … I had lunch with my mother," she said, her tone sounding off.

"Everything okay?" he asked.

"With her? Yes. It's just that…" She pulled away from him and pushed herself to a sitting position, comfortable with her nudity around him. "I asked her why your parents left their jobs, and she knew the same story I did. She had no idea that my dad accused your mother of stealing. I swear, Derek, she didn't know, not any more than I did."

He blew out a long breath. "It's in the past," he said, because it had to be. For both their sakes.

"Well, she knows now that my father lied. That he did something awful to your parents," she said, her eyes glistening with unshed tears. "She admitted that my father doesn't always play by the rules, and she said you overlook a lot in a marriage or a relationship, but I don't believe that." She met his gaze, searching for answers.

"I don't believe it either." He'd been debating on whether or not to tell her he'd had her brother investigated, and she'd just answered his question for him.

If he wanted her to trust him, he couldn't lie, not

even by omission. "I had a private investigator look into your brother's actions for the last year."

She blinked. "What? Why?"

He rolled his shoulders. "I can honestly tell you I'm not sure. Something is bothering me. I can't put my finger on it but I don't like him. I don't like how he treats you, I don't trust him with the company you love. I wish to hell I could tell you what I'm looking for, but I can't."

"Wait. You did it for me?" she asked, eyes wide. Disbelieving.

*Tell her the rest of it,* a voice in his head said. He drew a deep breath. "I also did it for me. You see, a few months ago, before we reconnected, I made an offer to buy Storms Consolidated."

"What?" She grabbed the pillow behind her and pressed it against her chest, covering herself. Comforting herself. "I thought the offer came from a large company."

"A shell corp. Your father never would have sold to me. Turns out he wouldn't have sold at all."

She curled her hands into the soft fabric of the pillow. "You tried to buy my company. And now you're having Spencer investigated so what? You can find dirt on him so you can grab the business another way?"

He reached out and tucked her hair behind her ear. "When you first showed up in my office, that was exactly my intention."

"You're not sitting here naked, telling me you used me."

"No, I'm spilling my guts because, as you said, you don't believe you should have to overlook a lot in a relationship. I don't want to give you any reason to walk away."

She tipped her head. "So…"

"So I wanted the company and not for the best reasons … until … you. Now I just want you happy, and if that means looking into your brother's past and his inability to run the company instead of you, so be it."

She opened her mouth, then closed it again. "Derek."

He placed a finger over her lips. "Shh. Let it go. If there's anything I think you need to know, I'll share it. Fair enough?"

She nodded. "Thank you," she whispered, tossed the pillow, and tackled him to the mattress, pressing kisses over his face, his neck, and moved lower.

They almost missed dinner being delivered.

# Chapter Eleven

C ASSIE WAS NERVOUS. She and Derek were on the way to meet with his mother, and butterflies had taken up residence in her stomach. Although Marie West had been a warm, wonderful woman and Cassie doubted that had changed, what she now knew about her father's behavior made today awkward. Cassie wasn't responsible for her dad's choices, but she felt sick anyway.

"Hey." Derek reached over the center console of his SUV and placed a hand on her jean-clad knee. "What's wrong?"

"What if she blames me? She should blame me. She should hate my whole family!"

"Cass, my mother doesn't have it in her to hate anyone. Least of all the woman who makes her son happy." He turned toward her and winked before returning his gaze to the road.

She breathed out and tried to relax. Thirty minutes and some traffic later, he pulled off at the exit. They ended up in a nice neighborhood with an eclectic mix of homes, some old, others renovated with new windows and siding.

He pulled up and parked in the driveway of one of the newer-looking homes, with white clapboard paint and black shutters.

"Ready?" he asked.

"Yep."

He came around to the side of the car and walked with her up the walk, ringing the doorbell. A few seconds later, a familiar woman opened the door. Marie had a few more wrinkles on her skin, a couple of strands of gray in her dark hair, and a wide, welcoming smile on her face.

"Derek, Cassandra! Come in, come in!"

After they stepped in out of the cold, Cassie found herself enveloped in a big hug. "It's so good to see you again," Derek's mother said.

"I feel the same way." She stepped back and smiled at Marie.

She hugged Derek next. "Let me take your jackets."

Marie hung their coats in the front hall closet and led them back to the kitchen. The inside of the house was a new as the outside, a beautifully decorated dark wood kitchen with state-of-the-art appliances. Marie had always loved to cook, so Cassie assumed this room got a lot of use.

The three sat at the kitchen table, a slice of home-made lemon meringue pie and coffee in front of each person. Good memories returned, of Marie giving her homemade treats after school, with milk instead of caffeine.

She dug into the pie. The lemony tart taste explod-ed on her tongue and she moaned. "Delicious."

At the sound, Derek shot her a warning look.

She snickered to herself. She hadn't meant to make an arousing noise, especially in front of his mom, and she cleared her throat.

"Mom, I thought I'd go change some of the higher ceiling lights while you two talk." He rose and took a long sip of coffee before starting to walk out.

"Be careful on the ladder," Marie said.

Derek all but rolled his eyes. "I will." He winked at Cassie and disappeared out the kitchen entry.

This man, she thought, well aware of the growing feelings she had for him. And just look how far they'd come, her sitting in his mother's kitchen.

Cassie knew how hard it was for him to leave her alone with his mother. But he had. Which meant he trusted her, she thought, her heart full.

She turned to Marie, who studied her through wise

eyes. "Thank you for seeing me," Cassie said.

"Are you kidding? From the time Derek mentioned your name, I couldn't wait to see what a fine young lady you grew into."

Cassie blinked in surprise. "You really don't … hold it against me? What my father did?"

"Honey, we aren't responsible for the sins of others."

"I'm so sorry. I'm also grateful you feel that way. You were a big part of my childhood, and it would break me if you hated me now."

Marie grabbed her hand. "On to other things, really."

"Okay. Okay." She sniffed before she could break down.

"So Derek tells me you're writing a series of articles about him." She leaned back in her seat.

Cassie rubbed her hands together, her excitement over her choice assignment coming through. "I'm almost ready to start working on them. I just need your perspective on what he was like as a child, how he's changed, if he has. Things like that."

"Well, let's see, he was a handful as a toddler, into everything." Marie smiled at the memories. "But he was also a good boy. He wanted to please both me and his father. Always willing to help around the house and at work."

Cassie took mental notes of everything Marie said. So far none of it surprised her. Derek was a decent man who took care of his friends and family, but he also had no problem digging into things he had no business doing … like her brother's life.

She blew out a puff of air. Since he'd been truthful with her, she'd tried to be grateful for his honesty and not angry he'd gone digging. Especially since he'd had good reasons. Reasons that included taking care of *her*. Cassie had been, and still was, torn by that revelation. She shouldn't have any loyalty to her family. After all, they'd shown her how little she mattered to them. But how did you throw away a lifelong belief of what family was supposed to mean?

Yet how could she blame Derek for anything he did before he'd been involved with her, or for looking into her brother's past indiscretions?

"Cassandra, what's wrong? You haven't heard a word I've said." Marie broke into her thoughts.

Cassie blinked and focused on the woman in front of her. "I'm sorry. I guess I have a lot on my mind. Let's get back to Derek."

The other woman nodded.

For the next twenty minutes, they talked about a variety of things. Derek's grades—all As, his preference for math and the sciences, lack of athletic ability as a child, him finding the gym and boxing and building muscles as an adult. And his desire to give back now that he had so much. It was interesting to get his mother's perspective on her son. She was obviously proud as she should be. She'd raised a wonderful man.

They talked about how losing his father had both hurt and defined him. He'd channeled the pain into a drive to succeed to make his father proud and provide for his mother to make up for the loss.

"He also nursed anger I wasn't aware of until recently," Marie said pointedly.

"At my father?" Cassie asked.

Marie nodded. "He believed that had we not been let go, we would have had health insurance and his father might have survived. What he doesn't understand—or didn't until I told him—was that his father was a stubborn mule. Who's to say he'd have gone to a doctor in time?"

Cassie nodded. "I understand your point and it's generous. Really."

"Don't get me wrong. I don't appreciate being accused, blamed, arrested for something I didn't do. I've lived with that pain and stigma all my life, but I've dealt with it. I think Derek is still learning."

As Marie spoke, guilt and embarrassment suffused Cassie. "I'm sorry," Cassie murmured again. It was all she could do.

The very thought that her father had lied ate away

at her as Marie patted her hand.

Cassie was determined to find out why her father had lied and damaged a good woman's reputation, even if she had to confront him herself. She knew her mother would never do it.

AFTER LEAVING HIS mother's, Derek drove by the high school he'd attended. As it turned out, school was closed for a Superindent's Day, but the janitor remembered Derek and was happy to let them take a walk around. Cassie wanted to see where he'd spent his formative years, as she called them, and he figured why the hell not?

Although he'd been busy changing high hat light bulbs for his mom, he'd also spent time eavesdropping on the women. His mother had been her usual kind self, but she'd been honest, too, when Cassie mentioned her father. And though it was a fair conversation, Derek had felt Cassie's discomfort, which way outweighed his mother's pain. She had clearly overcome the past. Derek had made more progress recently.

For Cassie it was still raw. Nothing but time and, maybe someday, an explanation would help.

After they strode down the halls with the now green lockers and he'd pointed out the science lab, they ended up in what used to be the computer lab. These days, the classrooms had smartboards and were much more high-tech. Kids had computers and laptops at home. Derek didn't know what the kids at this school could afford, but it was obvious things had been upgraded well.

"Can you imagine if we'd gone to school together?" Cassie asked, looking around the room that was now a normal classroom.

"Maybe I'd have had more time to get you to notice me," he said with a wink.

"Oh, I'd have noticed you," she murmured, wrapping her arms around his neck.

"Yeah?" He rubbed his nose against her cold one. "Think you'd have been brave enough to sneak a kiss?"

"I'd regret it if I didn't because now I know what I'd be missing." She threaded her hand through his hair and looked into his eyes.

"Damn straight," he muttered, and covered her lips with his, sliding his tongue into her mouth. She opened eagerly, and the kiss went on for a good long while, long, seductive sweeps of their tongues, meshing of mouths, and more.

His heart pounded hard in his chest as he pulled away. After the last twenty-four hours, Derek knew one thing for sure. He wasn't falling in love with her.

He was already there.

It didn't matter what her family thought, what had happened in the past between them. All that mattered was her.

"I love you," he heard himself say, unable to hold the words back now that he'd acknowledged them.

Her eyes opened wide. "You do?"

A smile pulled at his lips. "You don't believe me?"

She leaned back, her arms around his neck holding her steady. "No, I do. Want to know why?"

He cocked an eyebrow, wanting to hear her say it. "Why?"

"Because I love you too."

The words wrapped around his heart. Damn, he'd never have believed it. If, back when he'd gone to this school, someone had told him he'd find his other half in the princess across the yard, he'd have died laughing, sure someone was playing a joke on him. But what he felt for her was far from funny.

He kissed her again, locking his lips over hers and losing himself in her sweetness, tongues tangling. He nipped on her lower lip, and she pressed herself against him, jacket against jacket, heat sweeping through his body, his cock at attention.

This wasn't the best place for his declaration, but it was their place and he owned it. He swept his hand into her hair and kissed her again, hard and with urgency, until they heard a loud banging on the door.

"Come on, *kids*," the familiar voice of the janitor called. "Time to go."

He broke the kiss and laughed. "This could have happened way back when too."

She grasped his hand and met his gaze. "We'd have been too young to appreciate what we had," she said, her eyes warm and glazed with a combination of arousal and happiness.

"Point well made," he said. "We'd better get going or the janitor is going to drag us out."

She laughed and let him lead her out of the room, through the school, and into the frigid air.

DEREK SPENT THE night with Cassie in his bed. He made love to her slowly, savoring the feel of his cock bare inside her, sure of his feelings. Knowing she felt the same way. He'd never used those words with another woman before, and speaking them to Cassie felt right.

He didn't sleep much; he was too hyped up. He'd been open with Cassie. He'd been honest. And he finally had faith that they could work through the past on their terms. She wanted the same thing he did. To move on together.

He'd woken her earlier, his tongue between her

legs, tasting her, savoring her, bringing her over the edge, not once but twice before he found his way home, coming inside her. Losing himself in her and finding himself all over again.

Derek rose to light streaming through the window in his bedroom. The sun matched his mood. He'd never felt so light or free.

He was about to wake her up when his cell rang. He jumped up to get it before it woke her.

"Hello?"

"Derek, it's Kade."

"Hey. What's going on?" Because Kade didn't normally call this early. "Something with Blink?" Derek asked.

"No. You know how Lexie collects the articles we're all mentioned in?"

He rubbed the back of his neck, suddenly anxious. "Yeah?"

"You have a problem. I know you had faith in Cassie, but I told you to be careful."

The muscles in his neck bunched into tight knots. "Fucking spit it out," he muttered.

"There's an article on the *Take a Byte* website about you."

Derek shook his head. "That doesn't sound right. She would have told me." He glanced at the bed. Her bare shoulders peeked out from beneath the comforter; her brown hair was splayed across his pillow. So innocent-looking.

"Yeah? Would she also have told you she was going to do a trash piece on your mother?" Kade asked.

"Excuse me?" Derek asked, his voice rising.

Cassie jumped up, her bare breasts bouncing and teasing him before she grabbed the comforter and covered herself. "What's wrong?" She turned sleepy eyes on him.

He held up a hand, indicating she shouldn't interrupt. "Go on," he said to Kade.

"The story of how your mother worked for the Storms, was fired for stealing family jewelry, arrested … all of it laid out for the world to read."

His stomach clenched in dread. "Fuck. Thanks for the heads-up. I'll call you later." He turned to face Cassie.

"What is it?" she asked, concern in her voice.

"*Take a Byte* ran an article about me."

She blinked in surprise. "What? No. That's impossible."

"Well, somehow all the information about my past, growing up the son of the gardener and maid, my mother labeled a thief for stealing family jewelry, her firing and arrest, is out for public consumption. All of it," he said, his anger and fury rising with every word.

Her eyes opened wide. "What's the byline?" she

asked, jumping out of bed, bending down, and searching through her clothes. She popped up again with her phone in hand. "Byline," she said again. "Who wrote the article?" she asked, scrolling through her phone.

"Kade didn't say."

She studied her phone, gaze narrowing. "Anonymous. The byline says fucking anonymous." Frustration shook her body.

Her naked body, and he knew they had to get dressed. Before he could make the suggestion, she sat back down in bed and scrolled through her cell phone. "Dixon, it's Cassie. I know it's the weekend but it's urgent. Who wrote the article about Derek West, and why wasn't I informed first?"

She listened, her shoulders straightening as indignation rolled through her. "I'll kill him," she muttered. "Thanks," she said into the phone. "I'll be in touch."

She tossed her phone on the bed and met Derek's gaze. "I didn't write it."

"I know."

"But you thought it for a minute, didn't you?" she asked, hurt in her voice.

He shook his head. "In the second in which I found out, I didn't know what to think. All I knew was that my entire life had been revealed to the public by your magazine. I didn't connect any dots."

"Well, I didn't do it. I wouldn't." She pulled the

blanket up around her as a shield. "But I know who did. Dixon said they were told it was an executive decision and under no circumstances was I to be told. Or else jobs would be on the line." Her face was flushed with anger. "My brother. He's the only one with the ability to override me. The only one who could threaten job security and my people would believe him."

"Jesus," Derek muttered. The gall of the men in that family knew no bounds. He recalled his conversation with the PI. "Cassie, remember I told you if there was anything you needed to know about your brother, I'd tell you?"

She nodded, her shoulders slumping as she prepared herself for another blow. "What is it?"

"Your brother spent his time in Europe romancing women, then stealing from them."

"God." She rubbed her palms against her eyes before meeting his gaze. "I wonder if my father knows."

"I'm sorry, princess."

She shook her head, knowing what she had to do. "No. I'm sorry." She climbed out of bed and began to dress.

"What are you doing?" he asked, confused by her behavior.

She glanced up. "I'm going home. You need to help your mother cope with this mess. If she doesn't know, she needs to. And if she already knows, she's probably beside herself. And hating me," she muttered, pulling on her panties.

"Cassie, wait. Take a shower, think things through."

"Think what through? Without lifting a finger, I've destroyed your mother's life. That's what you get for going against your better instincts and letting me interview you. Letting me into your life."

"Hey." He strode over and grabbed her shoulders. "It wasn't you." Even as he'd heard the news, he hadn't jumped to that conclusion.

He knew her. He loved her. And she loved him, which meant she wouldn't deliberately hurt him.

"It might as well have been." She'd slid on her jeans and buttoned them, then pulled her sweater over her head. "I have to go confront Spencer. I can't let him run roughshod over my life. He has no right. He not only did a hit job on your mother but he undercut me. He knew I was planning a series on you, and he deliberately scooped me." She tossed her bag over her shoulder. "I want him to look me in the eye and tell me why. And then I am going to quit."

"Wait. What?"

She strode over to him, lifted herself onto her tip-toes, and pressed a kiss on his lips. A soft, fleeting kiss that felt suspiciously like good-bye. In a very final way.

"I'm sorry. Please tell your mother that too. I'm sorry that bringing me into your life caused such incredible pain."

"Cassie," he said in a deep voice he barely recognized. "What aren't you saying?"

She shook her head, eyes full of tears. "I need to go confront my brother. And you need to think about whether it's worth having me in your life, because I can guarantee you, Spencer won't stop if we're together. And you deserve a lot more than a life of humiliation." She started for the door.

And because he was stark naked and really did need to make sure his mother prepared for any fallout, he had no choice but to let Cassie go.

For now.

CASSIE WENT FROM flying on top of the world to dragging at the bottom. She couldn't believe her brother could do something so low, so underhanded ... so uncaring and awful. He'd betrayed his sister, hurt people Cassie cared about, and showed his true colors in a spectacular way.

She'd had one blissful night with Derek, sharing their feelings, believing in hope for the future, only to have everything shattered in the light of day.

She couldn't stay with him. She had to confront

her sibling, and Derek needed to think. She shuddered at the possibility of him leaving her, but could she really blame him if he did?

She left his place and took a cab to Penn Station, a train to her parents' local stop, and an Uber to the street she'd grown up on. The trip gave her time alone to think and stew, for her anger to brew and grow.

She went immediately to her old home, assuming she'd find her brother there. She banged on the door, hit the doorbell, and banged again, well aware her brother wasn't a morning person.

She started the process all over again, knocking hard on the door with her knuckles when Spencer flung the door open wide. He wore jeans and nothing else, his hair stood up on end, and he looked like he'd just rolled out of bed.

"Jesus, Cass, what the hell?"

She pushed past him and walked inside, not surprised to see in the short time he'd lived there he'd already put his own masculine touches on her once feminine home. Dark leather replaced her lighter touch, and there were no pretty plants around either. But this wasn't a call to discuss his choice in décor any more than it was a social call.

"How dare you. Where did you get the nerve to run a story in my magazine without my approval? And you chose the subject you knew I had plans for!" she said, her voice rising. "You played dirty. You went into the mud and rolled around in it with people I care about, in a magazine that isn't a gossip rag. How fucking dare you?" she asked, pushing hard at his shoulders to make her point.

"I need coffee for this," he muttered. Unfazed by her outburst, he turned his back on her and headed for the kitchen.

"Want coffee?" he asked, as if this were a normal morning between them.

"No! I want answers!"

He popped a K-Cup into his single coffee brewer and turned to face her. "It was a damn good article. Did you read it?"

"Oh my God." It was like dealing with her father but on steroids. Christopher heard and did what he wanted, and his son was no different, except Spencer left severe damage in his wake. "Let's take this one thing at a time. Why did you steal the subject of my article?"

"You snooze, you lose." The coffeemaker let out a hiss of steam, and Spencer turned to add milk to his cup. He swung back to her and raised his cup in a mock toast. "To me. Because you wouldn't have hit on the important points. You'd have extolled the virtues of the gardener's kid and ignored where he came from and the family scandal. In other words, all the good stuff."

It was obvious she wasn't going to get anywhere with him on the subject of poaching her article, so she turned to truthfulness instead. "Marie didn't steal from Mom."

Spencer took a sip of coffee. "What makes you so sure?"

"Because my gut tells me so. I trust her. I knew her and so did you! She was there for us growing up."

"Sit down, Cassie. I'm going to explain the facts of life to you," he said in a cool, condescending tone.

She blinked, taken off guard by his change in tone. She lowered herself into a chair at his table, listening only because she needed the information. Not because he'd told her what to do. "I'm listening."

"You're a Storms. He's nothing. Your loyalty is to your family, something you seem to have forgotten. I'm going to make sure you don't."

She narrowed her gaze. "Ignoring the elitist crap in what you said, what's your point?"

He shook his head. "So what if she didn't steal? She played an important role in protecting me. I took Mom's necklace. Dad jumped to the conclusion that it was Marie, and it was easier to let him believe it than to explain I'd pawned it."

Her mouth grew dry at his cavalier explanation. "Why? We have trust funds! Why would you need to steal from your mother?"

Spencer had the grace to look sheepish, his cheeks red. "I burned through it. I knew Dad would have a fit, so I took the necklace. Mom called from her trip and asked him to have it fixed, but it was missing Dad blamed Marie. Mom believed she'd misplaced it."

Cassie blinked. And blinked again, certain she was in an alternate universe. "And you let him," she whispered, horrified.

But then she remembered Derek's information on what Spencer had been up to while he was abroad, and his entire ugly existence was confirmed.

He was a selfish narcissist who believed he could do no wrong. That was the only explanation for Spencer's behavior. And as for her father, he hadn't deliberately framed an innocent woman, he'd believed his own actions to be justified.

"Why did Dad let me and Mom think they quit?" she asked.

"Because you and Mom have soft hearts. He said you would be devastated if you knew the truth, so he wove a lie you'd fall for." Spencer shook his head. "But Dad's way is not my way. I'm happy to tell you the truth now."

She pressed her pounding temples. "So you were against me seeing Derek because—"

"The same reasons I said. He's beneath you.

You're a Storms."

"And he's a constant reminder of what you did. You're also jealous because he's successful and you're a sycophant who lives off of others," she said in disgust.

Spencer didn't seem the least fazed by her description. He didn't care how he succeeded as long as he did.

She pushed herself to her feet, anger pulsing through her. "I'm through. Dad and Mom need to know the truth."

At least her mother did. Cassie wouldn't let her mom go on believing her husband had deliberately destroyed the lives of the West family. She'd looked broken when Cassie had told her. Defeated. At the very least, Cassie could restore her faith.

And maybe get Spencer out of his position of authority at Storms Consolidated while she was at it. Christopher had often covered for his son, but this was extreme. And Cassie had to believe he'd throw her brother out on his entitled ass once he knew.

"Dad won't care," Spencer said, full of confidence, contradicting her hopes. "He put me in charge. He wants me to succeed."

Yep. Narcissistic and a lot crazy. Cassie ignored him. Even if her father chose to ignore the past, the board would care. Somehow, someway, she'd save her grandfather's company from Spencer's destructive hands.

She had to. Because after today, the company might be all she had left.

FROM SPENCER'S, CASSIE headed next door to see her parents. Her father wasn't home, but her mother was happy to see her. She sat her down and explained the conversation she'd had with her brother. The truth brought her mother to tears. Relieved tears that her husband wasn't the monster they'd both feared, and angsty pain-filled tears that her son was capable of such callous, destructive behavior. Cassie hugged her mother, feeling all the same conflicting emotions, wishing there was something they could do to change the past. Knowing there wasn't anything that would undo the hurt Spencer had caused.

"You can't take on his behavior as your own," her mother said, squeezing both Cassie's hands tightly in her own.

"But I can make it easier on Derek's family to keep the past where it belongs. If they don't have to see me, to deal with our family in any way, they can put it behind them." Pain ripped through her chest, but they deserved better.

"Honey, I take it you're in love with the man or

you wouldn't be so emotional."

Cassie blinked back tears and nodded.

"Would you walk away from him if the situation were reversed? If his sibling had done something to me?" her mother asked.

"No. I'd fight for him."

"So why aren't you fighting for him now?" her mother asked.

"I told him to take time, to think. He deserves to make a decision about us with a clear head."

Her mother rolled her eyes. "Fine, but if he's a smart man, he won't let you go."

She laughed. "You're biased."

"Maybe, but I'm only speaking the truth.

She hugged her mother before easing back. "You'll talk to Dad? Tell him everything?"

Her mother nodded. "Oh, yes. I have every intention of having a long-overdue conversation with him about your brother. Among other things."

Cassie was about to stand when another question came to her. "The other day, when we met for lunch, you said you overlooked a lot. Did you mean it?"

A sigh escaped. "I suppose I meant we accept the person we love for who they are, flaws and all. Your father has many, especially as a parent. But he's not all bad. And I try to nudge him in the right direction when I can." She paused. "Does that help explain?"

Cassie nodded. "It does." She agreed that you had to accept the other person for who they were. But with her father's behavior, it still wasn't what she'd want in a relationship. But Cassie understood her mother better. "I love you," she said, hugging her mom again.

"Go live your life," her mother urged.

More than anything, Cassie wanted a life with Derek. At the very least, she wanted the chance to see if they could make it work long term. But first she needed to find a way to tell Derek what her brother had done.

And she needed time before she could decide how to do just that.

DEREK STOOD IN his mother's kitchen, a printed copy of the online *Take a Byte* article on the table. He paced the floor, unable to sit still, a host of emotions rushing through him. Anger at Spencer, frustration at his inability to do anything about the revelations. Once out there, there was nothing he *could* do to prevent readers from delving into his and his family's history.

And he worried about Cassie, because instead of sticking around, she'd rushed out, telling *him* to think about what having her in his life meant. As if he didn't already know. She meant everything to him. Nothing her brother did or said would change that.

"Sit down," his mother said, breaking into his thoughts. "You're nervous and it's driving me crazy."

Leave it to his mom to make him feel like a child again. He lowered himself into his seat. "Are you okay?" he asked her. "Will you have trouble facing your friends, dealing with people?" He worried about her, especially with his father gone.

"Derek, I hate to break it to you, but my friends don't read tech magazines, online or otherwise." She picked up the papers and ripped them in half.

He sputtered, shocked by her cavalier attitude. "What if the networks or other media outlets pick up on it?" he asked.

"This is my life. It has been for years. Do you think just because it's been made public it changes anything? I know I didn't do this. Anyone who cares about me knows I wouldn't do something like this. Other people can kiss my ass." Her eyes twinkled with amusement. "I'm over it. I have been for years."

She leaned over and grasped his hand. "I just wish I'd realized sooner that you weren't."

"Since Dad died, well, since Dad got sick, I've felt responsible."

"You can't put the world on your shoulders." She patted his hand. "I'm not your responsibility, though I love you for looking out for me. And I appreciate you showing me this article in case it pops up in other places. I told you to let the past go."

He managed to smile. "I have. Honestly."

"Has Cassandra? How is she dealing with this?" his mother asked.

"Not well. For her this was a personal attack too. Her brother knew she was planning to write a series about me. He undermined her intentionally. Not to mention, she feels guilty that the past is being dredged up again. She wants us to take a break so I can think about whether she's worth the aggravation." He shook his head, still unable to believe she thought so little of them, of him, that she believed he'd walk away from her so easily.

His mother's mouth dropped open. "You aren't seriously doing that, are you?"

"Of course not. But I do need to somehow convince her she isn't responsible for this. That neither you nor I hold it against her."

"You young people. You make life so difficult. Overthink everything." His mother waved a hand through the air. "Go get your girl."

Derek smiled. It wasn't as simple as his mother would like to believe. On the other hand, he didn't intend to let her break them apart over her brother's behavior either.

DEREK TRIED TO reach Cassie, but she'd turned off her phone. He spent the day hanging with Oscar, meeting his friends for dinner because they were worried and wanted to make sure he and his mother were okay.

The next day, he showed up at the office and texted her again before diving into work. He couldn't concentrate, not since he hadn't heard from Cassie, but he did his best to keep busy.

But no matter what, he was definitely heading to her place after work. Her time for ignoring him was over. And he damn well didn't need any thinking time.

By the time Becky told him he had a visitor who preferred not to give his name, Derek was grateful for the distraction. And curious.

He glanced up as the door opened, and Christopher Storms walked in. Nothing could have surprised Derek more.

He rose from his seat. He didn't know what the other man wanted, but he knew to meet him on equal footing.

"I see from your expression you recognize me," Christopher said.

"I lived on your property for a long time." And he hadn't changed much.

His hair was thinner, his face more lined, and he could now see he and Cassie shared the same coffee-brown eyes.

"True." Christopher inclined his head. "Can we sit?"

Derek nodded and lowered himself back into his chair. The back of his neck prickled uncomfortably. "What can I do for you?" he asked stiffly.

"When was the last time you spoke to my daughter?" Christopher asked.

Derek gripped his chair arms tightly. "Why is that your business?"

"Hang on." Christopher held up his hands in a sign of entreaty. "Believe it or not, I'm on your side."

"Explain."

He ran a hand over his beginning-to-bald head. "Cassie came to see her mother. She was beside herself because her brother wrote an article about you. One that went after your mother, revealing our whole sordid past."

Derek swallowed hard. And waited.

"She also told her something Spencer revealed. That *he* was the one who stole the necklace I accused your mother of taking."

Derek reared back in his seat. "Excuse me?"

"My son stole the necklace I accused your mother of taking."

"Stealing," Derek spat.

Christopher's face turned ruddy. "In my defense, I

really believed she'd stolen it."

"Guess you're a poor judge of character," Derek muttered, leaning forward on his desk. So far the information was interesting but didn't warrant this visit. "So why are you here?"

"I can't make it up to you, what I did to your mother. And the fact is, as my wife reminded me, I haven't been a particularly good father to Cassie." He shook his head, lowering it in shame. "I didn't know what to do with a girl." Yet another lame explanation. "Consider this as my way of making up for it. For a lot of things."

"What is?"

He shifted in his seat. "A couple of months ago, we received an offer on Storms Consolidated. From a company I'd never heard of."

Derek narrowed his gaze. "And?"

"I hired people to dig deeper. And I discovered that *you* made the offer. And I'm here to accept."

Derek's head spun. He braced his hands on his desk and leaned in. "Why?" He didn't trust any offer this man made.

Christopher leaned forward in his seat. "Because my wife tells me my daughter loves you. And I've screwed up enough for one lifetime. It's time to make things right."

Derek swallowed hard. He had no pity for Cassie's

father, but he was her parent. And Derek would do anything for another day with his own father.

So he looked the other man in the eye and said the only thing he could to his offer. "I accept."

CASSIE SPENT THE entire day in her bed, working on her laptop. If anything good was going to come of her brother's confession, Derek's mother would be exonerated, and to Cassie, that meant everything. Only after she'd finished the words could she go to Derek. She didn't know if they had a future, but without the words, she couldn't bring herself to try.

The phone rang in her apartment and she answered. "Hello?"

"Ms. Storms, this is Curt, the doorman at the front desk. There's a limo driver here for you."

"I'm sorry, what?"

"I'm going to put the man on the phone if that's okay with you."

Curious, she agreed. "Go ahead. Thank you."

"Ms. Storms, Mr. West sent me. My instructions are to wait for you to change into something nice and take you to meet him for dinner."

Shock and pleasure rippled through her in equal measure. He'd beat her to reaching out. Well, she could live with that. She had a lot to tell him, and she hoped he'd both understand and forgive. It had taken her awhile to hear what her mother had said and, more importantly, to accept it.

If the situation were reversed, if his family had hurt hers, she wouldn't hold it against him. Hopefully this overture meant he felt the same way.

She hit save on her document, shut her laptop, and headed for the shower. The driver was waiting, and she had to freshen up quickly.

She chose the same white cashmere dress she'd worn the night of their first date, left her hair down the same way, and clasped the same gold chain around her neck. She hoped her choices would evoke good memories for him.

They did for her.

After applying her makeup and a spritz of perfume, she headed downstairs. Her stomach flipped with nerves, similar to the way they'd done that first night.

She wasn't surprised when the limo pulled up to the restaurant of their first date. They were on identical wavelengths.

As the car parked, Derek stepped out of the front door of the restaurant. He met her at the curb. Helped her out of the backseat.

"You look beautiful," he said as his hand clasped hers.

Her gaze swung to his. "Thank you," she murmured. "You must be freezing." He wore a pair of black pants and a white dress shirt, no jacket.

"It's fine. Come. I reserved a private room in the back," he said, a grin pulling at his sexy mouth.

"Derek! You didn't have to do that again. But I'm glad you did."

He led her inside though she knew the way, and walked to the back room. Their booth was there and they sat side by side, his thigh close to hers. Just being near him, inhaling his cologne, taking in his handsome profile, she knew what she wanted.

She desired Derek and a future with him.

The waiter came to take their order. "Same as first time?" he asked.

"Sounds perfect to me." She was definitely in the mood for their steak au poivre, a baked potato loaded with sour cream, and creamed spinach.

Derek grinned her. "Me too."

Without looking at the wine menu, he ordered a bottle of Miner Cabernet. The red wine had been delicious with their meal.

"I'm assuming that's okay? If you still like wine, that is?" he asked with a wink before the waiter took his leave.

Her lips lifted in a knowing grin. She remembered her exact words here too. "I still prefer wine to beer.

Though once in a while, sharing a bottle can be fun."

Derek laughed, obviously pleased.

The waiter tilted his head and excused himself, pulling the door closed behind him, but he returned quickly and poured their wine, pausing for the ritual tasting.

Finally, though, they were alone.

"Well," she said into the silence.

"Well." He raised his glass. "To … us."

Before she tapped her glass to his, she wanted him to know everything. She lowered the glass. "There are things I think you ought to know first."

He raised an eyebrow. "Let me make this easy on you. Your brother was the one who stole the necklace, not my mother."

"How do you know that?"

He leaned in close, wrapping an arm around her shoulders. "I had a visitor. Someone else who wanted to make things right."

Her mouth went dry. "Who?"

"Your father."

She swallowed wrong and began to cough. She picked up the water and took a few sips, waiting until she could speak again.

"Are you okay?" Derek asked.

She managed a nod. "I don't understand."

"Apparently, your mother had a long talk with him

following *your* discussion with her."

"What did he say?"

"Believe it or not, he told me Spencer stole the necklace."

"Did he apologize?" she asked hopefully.

Derek let out a laugh. "No, I wouldn't say that. Not specifically. He did, however, excuse his behavior by saying he really had thought my mother took the jewelry. And then he said he wanted to make things right. With you and with my family.

Cassie's insides were trembling at the thought of Derek meeting with her father. "How?" she whispered.

"To make up for being a bad father to you, and to make things right by me, he accepted the offer I made on the company all those months ago."

Her head was spinning with the information Derek had given her and the implications of it all. "Slow down. How did he know you made the offer?"

"Investigation."

"Does that mean Spencer's no longer chairman?"

Derek nodded, the pleasure he got from that change evident in the broad smile on his face. "Your father hadn't yet finalized your brother's transfer of power in writing. He was still in charge of the company, and of course, he still holds majority stock. He can make any decision he chooses. And he chose to sell to me. I, in turn, chose to throw your brother out on his entitled ass."

"I'm speechless," she murmured.

"Good, because I'm not finished. I have more to say."

She blinked, sensing something big was coming. "What is it?" she asked.

"I'm signing the company over to you."

"What? You can't do that!" she said, her hands beginning to shake.

"I can. I only wanted it as a means of revenge. Storms Consolidated means everything to you. This way nobody can take it away from you ever again."

Tears leaked out of her eyes. "Derek, no. That's too generous. Beyond generous. Put me in charge if you want. I won't argue. I'll step up and make you money on your investment. That's all I really want."

He unwound his arm from behind her and turned so they were face-to-face. "You told me to think about what it meant to have you in my life. And that's all I've done since you shut me out."

"I didn't…" She closed her mouth. Opened it again. "I did. But I needed you to consider how you felt about the baggage that came with me."

He shook his head. "Silly woman. Does my past come along with me? My family?"

"Yes."

"And if things were reversed, would you walk away from me?"

She shook her head. "Of course not." She furrowed her brows, her forehead wrinkling. "I was being ridiculous."

"You could say that." He tapped her nose.

"I panicked. I spent the entire day working on a rebuttal article to what Spencer printed. I laid out the truth of what happened, with my brother's faults and lies."

"Princess, you can't prove he did it. He could sue you for libel. Your best bet is to let my kicking him to the curb suffice as his punishment. That and I'm sure your father isn't going to be funding his lifestyle anymore," Derek said, sounding satisfied with that outcome.

"I can live with that."

"Good. Now, I have a solution to you not wanting to let me gift the company to you."

Her heart was beating rapidly in her chest, her love for this man growing exponentially with every word that came out of his mouth. Nobody had ever looked out for her before. Put her first. Cared about what she wanted in life and gone out of their way to make sure she got it.

"What's your solution?" she asked.

He grasped her hand and held it tight in his. "Cassie Storms, I love you and someday I plan on marrying you. I realize it's too soon, and we have a long way to go getting to know each other better and building something solid and real. But when I do make you my wife, what's mine is yours. And then, you'll take the company as a wedding gift."

Her breath caught in her throat. Again. "Derek," she said, hardly able to believe the words coming out of his mouth.

"Not what I want to hear. 'Yes, Derek. I agree,' is about all I'll accept."

Her heart felt full to bursting. "Yes, Derek, I agree." She laughed and wrapped her arms around his neck and pulled him close. "Because I love you too. And I can't wait to spend my days … and nights with you. To build memories and work toward a future," she said, happy tears building behind her eyes.

He slid his hand behind her head, pulling her close. "Promise me you'll never pull away again. We have an issue, we talk it through."

She nodded. "I just wanted you to make a clear, rational choice."

"Well, I did. And I choose you," he said and sealed his lips over hers.

# Epilogue

LUCAS AND MAXIE'S wedding was taking place at a beautiful catering hall just outside of the city with windows all around, revealing the snow-covered trees and grass beyond the glass.

Kendall Parker sat in a chair by the floral-laden arch, surrounded by a small amount of family and friends, waiting for the procession to start. She was thrilled for Maxie, finally getting the happy ending she deserved, just as she was happy for her sister, happily married to Kade.

Kaden Barnes was a good man. He'd forgiven her when he could have caused a lot of trouble in her life. And her life was already difficult enough. Kade had understood that. And she would be forever grateful.

Before she could muse further, Cassie, Derek's girlfriend, joined her, taking the seat beside her.

"Hi."

"Hi," Kendall said. She'd met Cassie at a fundraiser, and Kendall liked the other woman.

Now that she was with Derek, Kendall figured she'd be seeing a lot more of her.

"Don't you just love weddings?" Cassie asked, her voice high-pitched with excitement.

"They're wonderful," Kendall murmured. And they always seemed to happen to other people.

Always a bridesmaid, she thought, but today she wasn't even that. Her twin was closer with Maxie. Kendall, on the other hand, had a problem keeping people in her life, maintaining close relationships.

Thank you, bipolar disorder. Then again, she hadn't been with a guy since she'd gotten the right kind of treatment and dedicated herself to her recovery. She hadn't been interested in any man since Julian.

"Are you okay?" Cassie asked.

"Just thinking … about relationships," Kendall said honestly.

"About Julian?" Cassie asked. It wasn't a leap considering the first time they'd met and really talked, Julian had shown up at the same fundraiser Kendall was attending.

Cassie had taken Kendall out of the room to calm her down while the others had seen to Kade, who always tended to explode when his ex-friend showed up. Kade looked out for Kendall like a big brother, and after what Julian had done, he didn't want the man anywhere near her.

He didn't have to worry. Kendall didn't want anything to do with the man who'd deliberately dated her, used her, set her up to hurt Kade and her sister. And because Kendall hadn't been on the right medications, hadn't cared who she hurt when she was on a high, she'd fallen right into Julian's trap.

Unfortunately she'd fallen in love with him too. Something else she did too easily, too fast, too impulsively. In Julian's case, she'd fallen for the man he'd pretended to be in order to get her to do his bidding. She was just reaching the point where she was getting over him.

"Kendall?" Cassie placed a hand on her arm and glanced at her with concern in her eyes.

"I'm sorry. I'm fine. And no, I'm not thinking about Julian."

Cassie blew out a relieved breath.

She'd probably been well briefed by Derek on Julian's behavior. About how stupid Kendall had been to fall for him.

The good news was she was well-medicated, holding down a job, living her life, making friends, not alienating people.

Suddenly music started, and Kendall turned toward the back of the room in time to see the groomsmen start down the aisle. Kade, wearing a tuxedo, walked with Lexie, who looked beautiful in a pale blue bridesmaid's dress. Next came Derek and Maxie's friend, Bailey, followed by the groom. Lucas strode down the aisle and turned to wait for his bride.

The music changed to the traditional "Here Comes the Bride," and Maxie stepped onto the carpeted aisle, framed by drapes on either side.

Kendall pivoted in time to catch Lucas's expression as he viewed the woman he loved in her ivory gown, her blonde hair falling in curls around her shoulders and the small swell of a baby bump at her stomach. A huge smile lit his face, and Kendall sighed at the love she saw there. A lump formed in her throat, and she had tears in her eyes, so happy for the couple she'd come to know.

Someday, she thought, reminding herself that she'd been working so hard to live a well-functioning life. She knew what she had to do, keep to her routine, healthy diet, exercise, and avoidance of stress. Not to mention keeping up with her therapy appointments. If she did all this, she thought, listening to the wedding vows, she had to believe that, someday, the happiness Kade and Lexie, Maxie and Lucas, and now Derek and Cassie had found could be hers, as well.

Thank you for reading GOING DOWN HARD. I hope you enjoyed. Get the next Billionaire Bad Boy's story (Julian and Kendall's story) in
GOING IN DEEP.

**Billionaire Bad Boys:**
**Rich, Powerful and sexy as hell.**

He isn't Mr. Nice Guy...

Julian Dane thought he'd hit rock bottom—until he met a woman (isn't that what they all say?). He used her and broke her heart. Now he wants to turn things around but the damage he dealt stands in his way.

Kendall Parker's unique issues have made it hard to live a normal life. Very few people understand her and she trusts even less ... but she believed in Julian once, and he only betrayed her.

Now Julian is back—a new man—and determined to win Kendall's heart. But this reformed bad boy just might find that Going in Deep is harder than it looks.

Meet the Dares!

Dare to Love – Book 1 Dare to Love Series –
(Ian Dare)

Want even more Carly books?
CARLY'S BOOKLIST by Series – visit:
www.carlyphillips.com/books

Sign up for Carly's Newsletter:
www.carlyphillips.com/newsletter-sign-up

Carly on Facebook:
www.facebook.com/CarlyPhillipsFanPage

Carly on Twitter:
www.twitter.com/carlyphillips

Hang out at Carly's Corner! (Hot guys & giveaways!)
smarturl.it/CarlysCornerFB

## CARLY'S MONTHLY CONTEST!

Visit: www.carlyphillips.com/newsletter-sign-up and enter for a chance to win the prize of the month! You'll also automatically be added to her newsletter list so you can keep up on the newest releases!

### Billionaire Bad Boys Reading Order:

Book 1: Going Down Easy

Book 2: Going Down Fast

Book 3: Going Down Hard

Book 4: Going in Deep

**Dare to Love Series Reading Order:**

Book 1: Dare to Love (Ian & Riley)

Book 2: Dare to Desire (Alex & Madison)

Book 3: Dare to Touch (Olivia & Dylan)

Book 4: Dare to Hold (Scott & Meg)

Book 5: Dare to Rock (Avery & Grey)

Book 6: Dare to Take (Tyler & Ella)

*each book can stand alone for your reading enjoyment

**DARE NY Series (NY Dare Cousins) Reading Order:**

Book 1: Dare to Surrender (Gabe & Isabelle)

Book 2: Dare to Submit (Decklan & Amanda)

Book 3: Dare to Seduce (Max & Lucy)

*The NY books are more erotic/hotter books

Read on for an excerpt of **Dare to Love**,
Ian and Riley's story.

# Dare to Love

## Excerpt

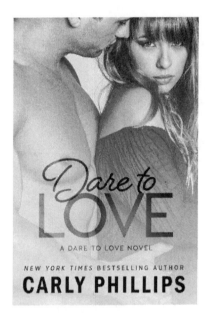

# Chapter One

ONCE A YEAR, the Dare siblings gathered at the Club Meridian Ballroom in South Florida to celebrate the birthday of the father many of them despised. Ian Dare raised his glass filled with Glenlivet and took a sip, letting the slow burn of fine scotch work its way down his throat and into his system. He'd need another before he fully relaxed.

"Hi, big brother." His sister Olivia strode up to him and nudged him with her elbow.

"Watch the drink," he said, wrapping his free arm around her shoulders for an affectionate hug. "Hi, Olivia."

She returned the gesture with a quick kiss on his cheek. "It's nice of you to be here."

He shrugged. "I'm here for Avery and for you. Although why you two forgave him—"

"Uh-uh. Not here." She wagged a finger in front of

his face. "If I have to put on a dress, we're going to act civilized."

Ian stepped back and took in his twenty-four-year-old sister for the first time. Wearing a gold gown, her dark hair up in a chic twist, it was hard to believe she was the same bane of his existence who'd chased after him and his friends until they relented and let her play ball with them.

"You look gorgeous," he said to her.

She grinned. "You have to say that."

"I don't. And I mean it. I'll have to beat men off with sticks when they see you." The thought darkened his mood.

"You do and I'll have your housekeeper short-sheet your bed! Again, there should be perks to getting dressed like this, and getting laid should be one of them."

"I'll pretend I didn't hear that," he muttered and took another sip of his drink.

"You not only promised to come tonight, you swore you'd behave."

Ian scowled. "Good behavior ought to be optional considering the way he flaunts his assets," he said with a nod toward where Robert Dare held court.

Around him sat his second wife of nine years, Savannah Dare, and their daughter, Sienna, along with their nearest and dearest country club friends. Missing were their other two sons, but they'd show up soon.

Olivia placed a hand on his shoulder. "He loves her, you know. And Mom's made her peace."

"Mom had no choice once she found out about *her*."

Robert Dare had met the much younger Savannah Sheppard and, to hear him tell it, fallen instantly in love. She was now the mother of his three other children, the oldest of whom was twenty-five. Ian had just turned thirty. Anyone could do the math and come up with two families at the same time. The man was beyond fertile, that was for damned sure.

At the reminder, Ian finished his drink and placed the tumbler on a passing server's tray. "I showed my face. I'm out of here." He started for the exit.

"Ian, hold on," his sister said, frustration in her tone.

"What? Do you want me to wait until they sing 'Happy Birthday'? No thanks. I'm leaving."

Before they could continue the discussion, their half brother Alex strode through the double entrance with a spectacular-looking woman holding tightly to his arm, and Ian's plans changed.

Because of *her*.

Some people had presence; others merely wished they possessed that magic something. In her bold, red dress and fuck-me heels, she owned the room. And he wanted to own her. Petite and curvy, with long, chocolate-brown hair that fell down her back in wild curls, she was the antithesis of every too-thin female he'd dated and kept at arm's length. But she was with his half brother, which meant he had to steer clear.

"I thought you were leaving," Olivia said from beside him.

"I am." He should. If he could tear his gaze away from *her*.

"If you wait for Tyler and Scott, you might just relax enough to have fun," she said of their brothers. "Come on, please?" Olivia used the pleading tone he never could resist.

"Yeah, please, Ian? Come on," his sister Avery said, joining them, looking equally mature in a silver gown that showed way too much cleavage. At twenty-two, she was similar in coloring and looks to Olivia, and he wasn't any more ready to think of her as a grown-up—never mind letting other men ogle her—than he was with her sister.

Ian set his jaw, amazed these two hadn't been the death of him yet.

"So what am I begging him to do?" Avery asked Olivia.

Olivia grinned. "I want him to stay and hang out for a while. Having fun is probably out of the question, but I'm trying to persuade him to let loose."

"Brat," he muttered, unable to hold back a smile at Olivia's persistence.

He stole another glance at his lady in red. He could no more leave than he could approach her, he thought, frustrated because he was a man of action, and right now, he could do nothing but watch her.

"Well?" Olivia asked.

He forced his gaze to his sister and smiled. "Because you two asked so nicely, I'll stay." But his attention remained on the woman now dancing and laughing with his half brother.

RILEY TAYLOR FELT his eyes on her from the moment she entered the elegantly decorated ballroom on the arm of another man. As it was, her heels made it difficult enough to maneuver gracefully. Knowing a devastatingly sexy man watched her every move only made not falling on her ass even more of a challenge.

Alex Dare, her best friend, was oblivious. Being the star quarterback of the Tampa Breakers meant he was used to stares and attention. Riley wasn't. And since this was his father's birthday bash, he knew everyone here. She didn't.

She definitely didn't know *him*. She'd managed to avoid this annual party in the past with a legitimate work excuse one year, the flu another, but this year,

Alex knew she was down in the dumps due to job problems, and he'd insisted she come along and have a good time.

While Alex danced with his mother then sisters, she headed for the bar and asked the bartender for a glass of ice water. She took a sip and turned to go find a seat, someplace where she could get off her feet and slip free of her offending heels.

She'd barely taken half a step when she bumped into a hard, suit-clad body. The accompanying jolt sent her water spilling from the top of her glass and into her cleavage. The chill startled her as much as the liquid that dripped down her chest.

"Oh!" She teetered on her stilettos, and big, warm hands grasped her shoulders, steadying her.

She gathered herself and looked up into the face of the man she'd been covertly watching. "You," she said on a breathy whisper.

His eyes, a steely gray with a hint of blue in the depths, sparkled in amusement and something more. "Glad you noticed me too."

She blinked, mortified, no words rushing into her brain to save her. She was too busy taking him in. Dark brown hair stylishly cut, cheekbones perfectly carved, and a strong jaw completed the package. And the most intense heat emanated from his touch as he held on to her arms. His big hands made her feel small, not an easy feat when she was always conscious of her too-full curves.

She breathed in deeply and was treated to a masculine, woodsy scent that turned her insides to pure mush. Full-scale awareness rocked her to her core. This man hit all her right buttons.

"Are you all right?" he asked.

"I'm fine." Or she would be if he'd release her so she could think. Instead of telling him so, she continued to stare into his handsome face.

"You certainly are," he murmured.

A heated flush rushed to her cheeks at the compliment, and a delicious warmth invaded her system.

"I'm sorry about the spill," he said.

At least she hoped he was oblivious to her ridiculous attraction to him.

"You're wet." He released her and reached for a napkin from the bar.

Yes, she was. In wholly inappropriate ways considering they'd barely met. Desire pulsed through her veins. Oh my God, what was it about this man that caused reactions in her body another man would have to work overtime to achieve?

He pressed the thin paper napkin against her chest and neck. He didn't linger, didn't stroke her anywhere he shouldn't, but she could swear she felt the heat of his fingertips against her skin. Between his heady scent and his deliberate touch, her nerves felt raw and exposed. Her breasts swelled, her nipples peaked, and she shivered, her body tightening in places she'd long thought dormant. If he noticed, he was too much of a gentleman to say.

No man had ever awakened her senses this way before. Sometimes she wondered if that was a deliberate choice on her part. Obviously not, she thought and forced herself to step back, away from his potent aura.

He crinkled the napkin and placed the paper onto the bar.

"Thank you," she said.

"My pleasure." The word, laced with sexual innuendo, rolled off his tongue, and his eyes darkened to a deep indigo, an indication that this crazy attraction she experienced wasn't one-sided.

"Maybe now we can move on to introductions. I'm Ian Dare," he said.

She swallowed hard, disappointment rushing through her as she realized, for all her awareness of him, he was the one man at this party she ought to stay away from. "Alex's brother."

"Half brother," he bit out.

"Yes." She understood his pointed correction. Alex wouldn't want any more of a connection to Ian than Ian did to Alex.

"You have your father's eyes," she couldn't help

but note.

His expression changed, going from warm to cold in an instant. "I hope that's the only thing you think that bastard and I have in common."

Riley raised her eyebrows at the bitter tone. Okay, she understood he had his reasons, but she was a stranger.

Ian shrugged, his broad shoulders rolling beneath his tailored, dark suit. "What can I say? Only a bastard would live two separate lives with two separate families at the same time."

"You do lay it out there," she murmured.

His eyes glittered like silver ice. "It's not like everyone here doesn't know it."

Though she ought to change the subject, he'd been open, so she decided to ask what was on her mind. "If you're still so angry with him, why come for his birthday?"

"Because my sisters asked me to," he said, his tone turning warm and indulgent.

A hint of an easier expression changed his face from hard and unyielding to devastatingly sexy once more.

"Avery and Olivia are much more forgiving than me," he explained.

She smiled at his obvious affection for his siblings. As an only child, she envied them a caring, older brother. At least she'd had Alex, she thought and glanced around looking for the man who'd brought her here. She found him on the dance floor, still with his mother, and relaxed.

"Back to introductions," Ian said. "You know my name; now it's your turn."

"Riley Taylor."

"Alex's girlfriend," he said with disappointment. "I saw you two walk in."

That's what he thought? "No, we're friends. More like brother and sister than anything else."

His eyes lit up, and she caught a glimpse of yet another expression—pleasantly surprised. "That's the best news I've heard all night," he said in a deep, compelling tone, his hot gaze never leaving hers.

At a loss for words, Riley remained silent.

"So, Ms. Riley Taylor, where were you off to in such a hurry?" he asked.

"I wanted to rest my feet," she admitted.

He glanced down at her legs, taking in her red pumps. "Ahh. Well, I have just the place."

Before she could argue—and if she'd realized he'd planned to drag her off alone, she might have—Ian grasped her arm and guided her to the exit at the far side of the room.

"Ian—"

"Shh. You'll thank me later. I promise." He

pushed open the door, and they stepped out onto a deck that wasn't in use this evening.

Sticky, night air surrounded them, but being a Floridian, she was used to it, and obviously so was he. His arm still cupping her elbow, he led her to a small love seat and gestured for her to sit.

She sensed he was a man who often got his way, and though she'd never found that trait attractive before, on him, it worked. She settled into the soft cushions. He did the same, leaving no space between them, and she liked the feel of his hard body aligned with hers. Her heart beat hard in her chest, excitement and arousal pounding away inside her.

Around them, it was dark, the only light coming from sconces on the nearby building.

"Put your feet up." He pointed to the table in front of them.

"Bossy," she murmured.

Ian grinned. He was and was damned proud of it. "You're the one who said your feet hurt," he reminded her.

"True." She shot him a sheepish look that was nothing short of adorable.

The reverberation in her throat went straight to Ian's cock, and he shifted in his seat, pure sexual desire now pumping through his veins.

He'd been pissed off and bored at his father's ridiculous birthday gala. Even his sisters had barely been able to coax a smile from him. Then *she'd* walked into the room.

Because she was with his half brother, Ian hadn't planned on approaching her, but the minute he'd caught sight of her alone at the bar, he'd gone after her, compelled by a force beyond his understanding. Finding out she and Alex were just friends had made his night because she'd provide a perfect distraction to the pain that followed him whenever his father's other family was near.

"Shoes?" he reminded her.

She dipped her head and slipped off her heels, moaning in obvious relief.

"That sound makes me think of other things," he said, capturing her gaze.

"Such as?" She unconsciously swayed closer, and he suppressed a grin.

"Sex. With you."

"Oh." Her lips parted with the word, and Ian couldn't tear his gaze away from her lush, red-painted mouth.

A mouth he could envision many uses for, none of them tame.

"Is this how you charm all your women?" she asked. "Because I'm not sure it's working." A teasing smile lifted her lips, contradicting her words.

He had her, all right, as much as she had him.

He kept his gaze on her face, but he wasn't a complete gentleman and couldn't resist brushing his hand over her tight nipples showing through the fabric of her dress.

Her eyes widened in surprise at the same time a soft moan escaped, sealing her fate. He slid one arm across the love seat until his fingers hit her mass of curls, and he wrapped his hand in the thick strands. Then, tugging her close, he sealed his mouth over hers. She opened for him immediately. The first taste was a mere preview, not nearly enough, and he deepened the kiss, taking more.

Sweet, hot, and her tongue tangled with his. He gripped her hair harder, wanting still more. She was like all his favorite vices in one delectable package. Best of all, she kissed him back, every inch a willing, giving partner.

He was a man who dominated and took, but from the minute he tasted her, he gave as well. If his brain were clear, he'd have pulled back immediately, but she reached out and gripped his shoulders, curling her fingers through the fabric of his shirt, her nails digging into his skin. Each thrust of his tongue in her mouth mimicked what he really wanted, and his cock hardened even more.

"You've got to be kidding me," his half brother

said, interrupting at the worst possible moment.

He would have taken his time, but Riley jumped, pushing at his chest and backing away from him at the same time.

"Alex!"

"Yeah. The guy who brought you here, remember?"

Ian cursed his brother's interruption as much as he welcomed the reminder that this woman represented everything Ian resented. His half brother's friend. Alex, with whom he had a rivalry that would have done real siblings proud.

The oldest sibling in the *other* family was everything Ian wasn't. Brash, loud, tattoos on his forearms, and he threw a mean football as quarterback of the Tampa Breakers. Ian, meanwhile, was more of a thinker, president of the Breakers' rivals, the Miami Thunder, owned by his father's estranged brother, Ian's uncle.

Riley jumped up, smoothing her dress and rubbing at her swollen lips, doing nothing to ease the tension emanating from her best friend.

Ian took his time standing.

"I see you met my brother," Alex said, his tone tight.

Riley swallowed hard. "We were just—"

"Getting better acquainted," Ian said in a seductive tone meant to taunt Alex and imply just how much better he now knew Riley.

A muscle ticked in the other man's jaw. "Ready to go back inside?" Alex asked her.

Neither one of them would make a scene at this mockery of a family event.

"Yes." She didn't meet Ian's gaze as she walked around him and came up alongside Alex.

"Good because my dad's been asking for you. He said it's been too long since he's seen you," Alex said, taunting Ian back with the mention of the one person sure to piss him off.

Despite knowing better, Ian took the bait. "Go on. We were finished anyway," he said, dismissing Riley as surely as she'd done to him.

Never mind that she was obviously torn between her friend and whatever had just happened between them; she'd chosen Alex. A choice Ian had been through before and come out on the same wrong end.

In what appeared to be a deliberately possessive move, Alex wrapped an arm around her waist and led her back inside. Ian watched, ignoring the twisting pain in his gut at the sight. Which was ridiculous. He didn't have any emotional investment in Riley Taylor. He didn't do emotion, period. He viewed relationships through the lens of his father's adultery, finding it easier to remain on the outside looking in.

Distance was his friend. Sex worked for him. It

was love and commitment he distrusted. So no matter how different that brief moment with Riley had been, that was all it was.

A moment.

One that would never happen again.

RILEY FOLLOWED ALEX onto the dance floor in silence. They hadn't spoken a word to each other since she'd let him lead her away from Ian. She understood his shocked reaction and wanted to soothe his frazzled nerves but didn't know how. Not when her own nerves were so raw from one simple kiss.

Except nothing about Ian was simple, and that kiss left her reeling. From the minute his lips touched hers, everything else around her had ceased to matter. The tug of arousal hit her in the pit of her stomach, in her scalp as his fingers tugged her hair, in the weight of her breasts, between her thighs and, most telling, in her mind. He was a strong man, the kind who knew what he wanted and who liked to get his way. The type of man she usually avoided and for good reason.

But she'd never experienced chemistry so strong before. His pull was so compelling she'd willingly followed him outside regardless of the fact that she knew without a doubt her closest friend in the world would be hurt if she got close to Ian.

"Are you going to talk to me?" Alex asked, breaking into her thoughts.

"I'm not sure what to say."

On the one hand, he didn't have a say in her personal life. She didn't owe him an apology. On the other, he was her everything. The child she'd grown up next door to and the best friend who'd saved her sanity and given her a safe haven from her abusive father.

She was wrong. She knew exactly what to say. "I'm sorry."

He touched his forehead to hers. "I don't know what came over me. I found you two kissing, and I saw red."

"It was just chemistry." She let out a shaky laugh, knowing that term was too benign for what had passed between her and Ian.

"I don't want you to get hurt. The man doesn't do relationships, Ri. He uses women and moves on."

"Umm, Pot/Kettle?" she asked him. Alex moved from woman to woman just as he'd accused his half brother of doing.

He'd even kissed *her* once. Horn dog that he was, he said he'd had to try, but they both agreed there was no spark and their friendship meant way too much to throw away for a quick tumble between the sheets.

Alex frowned. "Maybe so, but that doesn't change

the facts about him. I don't want you to get hurt."

"I won't," she assured him, even as her heart picked up speed when she caught sight of Ian watching them from across the room.

Drink in hand, brooding expression on his face, his stare never wavered.

She curled her hands into the suit fabric covering Alex's shoulders and assured herself she was telling the truth.

"What if he was using you to get to me?"

"Because the man can't be interested in me for me?" she asked, her pride wounded despite the fact that Alex was just trying to protect her.

Alex slowed his steps and leaned back to look into her eyes. "That's not what I meant, and you know it. Any man would be lucky to have you, and I'd never get between you and the right guy." A muscle pulsed in Alex's right temple, a sure sign of tension and stress. "But Ian's not that guy."

She swallowed hard, hating that he just might be right. Riley wasn't into one-night stands. Which is why her body's combustible reaction to Ian Dare confused and confounded her. How far would she have let him go if Alex hadn't interrupted? Much further than she'd like to imagine, and her body responded with a full-out shiver at the thought.

"Now can we forget about him?"

Not likely, she thought, when his gaze burned hotter than his kiss. Somehow she managed to swallow over the lump in her throat and give Alex the answer he sought. "Sure."

Pleased, Alex pulled her back into his arms to continue their slow dance. Around them, other guests, mostly his father's age, moved slowly in time to the music.

"Did I mention how much I appreciate you coming here with me?" Obviously trying to ease the tension between them, he shot her the same charming grin that had women thinking they were special.

Riley knew better. She *was* special to him, and if he ever turned his brand of protectiveness on the right kind of woman and not the groupies he preferred, he might find himself settled and happy one day. Sadly, he didn't seem to be on that path.

She decided to let their disagreement over Ian go. "I believe you've mentioned how wonderful I am a couple of times. But you still owe me one," Riley said. Parties like this weren't her thing.

"It took your mind off your job stress, right?" he asked.

She nodded. "Yes, and let's not even talk about that right now." Monday was soon enough to deal with her new boss.

"You got it. Ready for a break?" he asked.

She nodded. Unable to help herself, she glanced over where she'd seen Ian earlier, but he was gone. The disappointment twisting the pit of her stomach was disproportional to the amount of time she'd known him, and she blamed that kiss.

Her lips still tingled, and if she closed her eyes and ran her tongue over them, she could taste his heady, masculine flavor. Somehow she had to shake him from her thoughts. Alex's reaction to seeing them together meant Riley couldn't allow herself the luxury of indulging in anything more with Ian.

Not even in her thoughts or dreams.

# About the Author

Carly Phillips is the *N.Y. Times* and *USA Today* Best-selling Author of over 50 sexy contemporary romance novels featuring hot men, strong women and the emotionally compelling stories her readers have come to expect and love. Carly's career spans over a decade and a half with various New York publishing houses, and she is now an Indie author who runs her own business and loves every exciting minute of her publishing journey. Carly is happily married to her college sweetheart, the mother of two nearly adult daughters and three crazy dogs (two wheaten terriers and one mutant Havanese) who star on her Facebook Fan Page and website. Carly loves social media and is always around to interact with her readers. You can find out more about Carly at www.carlyphillips.com.

Made in the USA
San Bernardino, CA
04 March 2017